First Cousin Once Removed

by

Delia Drake

North Country Press

As always, this book is dedicated to my late husband Austin J. Brann Sr. and Adrian, my little helper, who has also passed on.

~

With thanks to Mikki Studley, my daughter, and Alana McCamish, my granddaughter, for always being there with love and encouragement.

Cast of Characters

TEMPLE MATHIEU, heroine, Chief Librarian of Susan Claire
Chadworth Library

Thea's Household at Rigby House:
MARCHIONESS TIMOTHEA CLAIRE CHADWORTH
TOTTERSHAM SANDERSON (THEA)
LIEUTENANT CLARK TRAFTON SANDERSON, Thea's
husband
PERRY DAWSON, Thea's father's half brother
ABBY WILLOWS, Thea's assistant
MRS. OLIVIA MCMILLIAN, the triplets' nanny
BARRY APPLEGATE, Chief of Security at Rigby House and
owner of Applegate Security
RENE GRENIER, Chef
GRETCHEN FULLER, housekeeper
TARDY BURGER, master groundskeeper and overall
factotum
PETER WELLS, bodyguard
JOE TALLEY, bodyguard
TOM HARDY, bodyguard
TRIPLETS, Lord Timothy Clark Sanderson-Tottersham
Lord Granger Chadworth Sanderson-Tottersham
Lord Trafton Perry Sanderson-Tottersham

Other Characters:
HAL CHADWORTH, Thea's mother's brother
WANDA CHADWORTH, Hal's wife
TONY CHADWORTH, Thea's first cousin
CARRY CHADWORTH, Thea's first cousin
EX-SENATOR AND JUDGE GRANGER
SANDERSON, Clark's father
SYLVIA SANDERSON, Clark's mother
PETER HAPPY "HAP" STURGIS

ARABELLA VERMILLION, Granger's sister, Clark's aunt
SENATOR FRANK VERMILLION, Arabella's husband
ANDREW VERMILLION, Clark's first cousin
MR. HENRY SEVERIED, Thea's lawyer and friend
HILLARY LEIGHTON, local spoiled rich girl
WEBSTER ADAMS, Temple's assistant
EMILY HARRISON, Thea's best friend
BRUCE GARRETT, Emmy's fiancé
DERRICK & HILDA HARRISON, Emmy's parents
RANCE FULLER, forensic deputy sheriff
ANSEL JORDAN, sheriff
PATRICK PHINNEY, owner of the Gull Restaurant
EARL SCANLON, Temple's stepfather
JEFF SCANLON, Temple's stepbrother
ERIC SCANLON, Temple's stepbrother

One

Temple Mathieu was running late as she slipped her key into the lock of the front door at the Susan Claire Chadworth Library. She had been head librarian now for two years and still got a thrill when she opened the door to "her" library. She had been appointed head librarian when the sponsor of the library, Thea Sanderson, Susan Chadworth's daughter, had retired to pick up a British title, and to give birth to a set of beautiful bouncing triplet baby boys with her husband Lieutenant Clark Sanderson of the county sheriff's office. They lived part of the time in Maine and part of the time in England. Temple had originally been a fill-in for Emily Harrison, who was Thea's second in command at the library, when Emmy had left to be with Thea and to help her find her mother and father's killer. It had all turned out well for Thea, and Emmy had since decided to put her attention full time to her relationship with her fiancé Bruce Garrett and his budding construction business. Bruce had just finished building the house that Temple now lived in. It was built on the same property where Thea's own little house had once stood. It had been burned to the ground by an arsonist a couple of years ago and Thea had decided to rebuild and had rented the house on Wheaten Street to Temple. Temple even drove the little VW that had once belonged to Thea—Thea had sold her the car for one dollar and she loved it.

Temple shook her head and said to herself, "Enough wool gathering. I have that new shipment of books to put out today as well as all my other duties. Webster won't be in until two o'clock today." Webster Adams was Temple's latest assistant, and he was working out well. He worked part time for her and part time for Mr. Severied, a lawyer in Rigby, a nearby town.

Temple went straight to her office to put her purse away and was shocked to find the door wide open. She always closed and locked her office door as the library safe was in there and it held valuable items that belonged to Thea. Temple cautiously approached the door and looked in. Blood covered just about every surface in the room. The body on the floor in front of Temple's desk was without a doubt very dead. Temple let out a squeak and backed away from the doorway. She raced outside and sat on the library steps and put her head between her knees. "I will not faint, I will not faint," she muttered. After a few minutes she reached into her purse that she had miraculously held onto, and pulled out her cell phone. She called the sheriff's department and told the dispatcher what she had found at the library. She then called Rigby House and asked to speak to Thea. She knew that Thea was in Maine for the summer at least, and she wanted her to know what was happening. Abby Willows, Thea's assistant could tell Temple was upset and went to get Thea who was just finishing spooning cereal into the mouths of her three sons. They were adorable triplets and very hard to tell apart but Thea, Abby, Clark and Perry Dawson could tell the difference by their personalities. Perry was Thea's uncle on her father's side. Abby, taking over with the triplets, told Thea that Temple was upset and needed to speak to her right away. Thea went to the phone and listened to Temple calmly tell her what she had found in her office when she got to the library a few minutes ago. Thea said, "Clark is still here, I will send him over right now. I think he just got the call from the sheriff's department anyway." She glanced at her husband who had just hurried into the room with a concerned look on his face.

"Wait!" Temple said. "Thea, the body on the floor is Carry Chadworth, your cousin."

"What!" shouted Thea. "Are you sure, Temple?"

"Yes, Thea, believe me I wish it wasn't so. I would know her anywhere."

"Okay, Temple, just hang in there. Help is on the way."

Clark gave Thea an inquiring look and she told him who the victim was. "Oh God, babe, I'm so sorry," he said. He gave her a hug, kissed the boys and left in a hurry.

Abby took the boys in to Mrs. McMillian so they would not get upset about their mother being distracted. Mrs. McMillian was their new nanny and she was wonderful with them. She lived in a small suite on the third floor of Rigby House and was always accessible to the boys.

Thea in the meantime prepared to travel to Trafton to speak to Carry's parents. Her Uncle Hal and his wife Wanda had raised her and she felt she should be the one to tell them about Carry.

Two

Temple sat on the steps of the library and waited for the police to arrive. She reflected on what she had seen. It looked like someone had slit Carry's throat and the blood had spurted all over the room. "The killer must be covered in blood," she thought. She had not liked Carry but it was terrible that she had died like that. The last time she had seen Carry was at the Gull yesterday at lunch time. The Gull was a busy little restaurant and most of the locals ate there. Temple had been talking with Barry Applegate at a small table and Carry made it her business to approach them. When Temple had told her they were having a private conversation, Carry tried to push Temple off her chair. Temple being a tall and elegant five nine was not easily pushed. She shoved Carry away from her and Carry landed on her rear end on the floor. Barry helped Carry up and told her to go on her way, but she was spitting mad at Temple and left shouting vitriolic poison. It had spoiled the nice chat she and Barry were having and they soon left, going their separate ways. Temple now thought about that ruckus that half the town had witnessed and thought she might want to call a lawyer. She had discovered the body and had just recently had a public altercation with Carry. It didn't look good for Temple. Add to that her prints would surely be on the bone-handled knife that was lying next to the body and she was probably in deep doo-doo.

The sheriff's department arrived in force and promptly took control of the library. A crowd was gathering and asking Temple questions that she declined to answer. Clark arrived from Rigby House and took charge. Temple knew he wouldn't jump to conclusions but had to face the facts. She also knew that she had to call Barry and let him know that the murder weapon also had his prints on it. It didn't look good for either one of them. Barry had been at the library Friday before lunch and they had been inspecting the antique bone-handled knife that Barry had donated to the display of artifacts for the Penobscot Native Americans. Barry was a Penobscot himself and was proud of his heritage. He was extremely handsome with jet black hair worn in a glossy braid down his back. He was about six feet four and carried himself with an innate grace. His complexion was dusky and smooth and he spoke in a cultured voice. He had graduated with distinction from Yale and owned his own business—Barry was also Chief of Security for Thea and Clark's estate. He and his three employees covered the estate full time and acted as body guards for the triplets wherever they went. He had been grades ahead of Thea, Emmy and Temple when they were in school and the girls had all had a wild crush on him. Temple thought him to be about thirty-four. Temple and Barry had both handled the razor sharp knife and if the killer had not erased their prints they would still be there. The knife and other artifacts had been mounted in a large glass shadow box in the office. She had not had a chance to put a lock on the glass door yet, but had not worried about it as she always kept the door locked. She wondered how the killer had gotten into the office. She was interrupted as Sheriff Jordan came and sat down beside her on the steps. He asked her specifically what she had done after discovering the body and she told him everything. He said she had been smart to get out of the library and asked her about the knife. She told him about Barry's contribution to the artifacts display and that she and Barry had both handled the knife just last Friday. He thanked her for the information and told her the library would be closed for a few days. Temple was allowed to go to her station at the front of the library and make up a notice to post for the patrons. The sheriff then told her to go home and that she would need to make a statement at his office later in the day.

Temple called Barry on her cell phone on her way home and told him what had happened. He was sympathetic about the mess but was not surprised about the victim.

"Carry was one very unpleasant lady and that is putting it politely," he said. "I will talk to Clark and the sheriff. Try not to worry, Temple, just go home and rest."

Three

Still Monday morning

Barry met Thea leaving the complex and asked if she needed him to accompany her to the Chadworths'. "No, Barry, I think they will need to be alone for a while. I will talk to Uncle Hal myself and let him tell Wanda and Tony." Barry expressed his sympathy to Thea for Carry and she said, "Thank you Barry, but we both know how Carry made enemies wherever she went. This won't be easy."

Barry told Thea what Temple had told him and she said, "Like I said before, this will be difficult for all of us. Carry is continuing to cause trouble even after her death."

"Thea," Barry said, "you don't know the half of it. Temple and Carry got into a shoving match at the Gull yesterday and Carry swore to get even. She left screaming that Temple thinks she is special just because she is your friend. What Temple won't tell you is, it started when Carry came to our table while we were having lunch and asked Temple if she was slumming with her redskin. She said that even her redskin wouldn't associate with her when people found out what she really was. Temple told her politely to shove off and then Carry tried to push Temple off her chair. Temple shoved her back and she landed on her ass in the middle of the Gull floor. I picked her up and told her to leave and that is when she started screaming all her threats."

Thea said, "I apologize for my cousin, Barry. She was very unhappy and mean. I think I would have liked to see Temple push her on her butt, but it complicates things right now. I do need to be on my way before Hal hears it from someone else. Catch you later. Please take care of my babies for me."

"Always, Thea," Barry said and saluted her on her way.

Thea drove carefully into Trafton and went right to the Chadworths' hardware store. She found Hal at the front counter waiting on a customer and waited until he was done, then asked if she could talk to him in his office.

"Always glad to talk to my favorite niece, but you're looking kind of peaked, little one. Are those boys of ours doing okay?" he asked.

"Yes, Uncle Hal, they are just wonderful and wanting to see you as usual. Uncle Hal, there is no easy way to tell you this, but I wanted to be the one to tell you. Carry was found murdered this morning at the library. I have no particulars for you other than the fact that she is dead and that she was killed by another hand. I will watch the store for you if you want to go tell Wanda and Tony."

Hal Chadworth's face had crumpled and tears were streaming down. "Thea, it was only a matter of time before that girl got herself killed. She had a mean streak a mile wide and I tried to help her, but there was no telling her anything. She was my daughter and I loved her in spite of her ugly ways. Thanks, Thea, but I will close the store for a couple days. Thank you for coming to tell me yourself. Now get back to those little men and hug them for me."

Thea left the store in tears herself. She shed them for Hal and Wanda because Carry would have scorned her for them. She had grown up in the same house as Carry but was as distant as a stranger with her. Carry had been just plain mean and she had some mean friends. In fact, you had to be mean to be Carry's friend. She headed for Temple's house to see what she could do to put Temple's mind at ease.

Four

Monday mid-morning

The sheriff had filled Clark in on what Temple had told him. They looked at each other and knew they had to find whoever did this in a hurry or Temple would be in trouble. They finished processing the scene and the coroner had done his thing with Carry. He estimated she had been dead about eight to twelve hours which put it at sometime around eight to midnight the night before. He hoped Temple would have an alibi for that time. Barry had an impeachable one—he had been playing cards with Clark, Rene and Perry all evening. Plus he had been on duty for the boys even though Clark and Perry were home. Many changes had taken place since the arrival of the little heirs and everyone was always on their guard.

When the body bag was taken out of the library the crowd tried to see who it was, but of course the face was covered. It wouldn't be long before the word would get out. Clark knew he had to act in a hurry to find the killer. He also knew he had to call his cousin Andrew and put him on retainer for Temple. Temple and Andrew were always at each other's throats and couldn't get along for five minutes, but Temple would need the best criminal lawyer around and Andrew Vermillion was it. He told Andrew what the situation was and Andrew said, "I am on it right now, Clark! I will take good care of her whether she likes it or not."

Having put that situation into capable hands, Clark put his mind to solving this murder. A window in the back of the library had been broken and that is how the killer got in. Clark figured that Carry was with whoever broke in and she had entered the library on her own free will. They had jimmied the lock on the office door and it was only after they had breached the office that the killing took place. It must have been a killing of opportunity as they hadn't brought a weapon with them, so probably premeditated murder was out for now. It was going to be hard to find the killer among

Carry's friends as they were all the "cover your butt" type and nobody would be doing any talking, that's for sure.

Clark and the sheriff left the library and headed for the office. They wanted to get going on the physical evidence as soon as possible. Clark had amassed a fortune's worth of equipment in his office to assist the department in solving crimes. They had their forensics expert run the prints on the knife, window and office. Not surprisingly, they contained Temple's prints. The whole library was awash with prints. Barry Applegate's prints were also on the knife as Temple had speculated and no one else had left any. Clark said, "Whoever killed her was obviously wearing gloves to break in. The pictures of the body show that Carry's hands are clean. There is blood everywhere else on her body so the killer must have removed them after she was dead. Carry didn't see it coming, she was probably too busy being her old obnoxious self. Now all we have to do is weed through the many people that would have liked to see Carry dead."

"Good luck with that," said the sheriff.

"Maybe Hillary Leighton can help you compile a list," said Rance Fuller, the forensics deputy. "They have been pretty chummy since Hillary came home."

"Like a bad penny she had to return," said Clark. "Good idea, Rance, you can get the list when you check her alibi."

The sheriff laughed and Rance groaned. "How come I get all the fun?" he asked.

Clark went back to the library to go back over the crime scene more carefully. He felt they were missing something, but he couldn't put his finger on it. There was still a guard on the door and Clark entered easily enough. It was pleasant in spite of the subdued atmosphere. He could see why the girls would go into the library profession. He knew that Thea missed her books and people. She filled in occasionally when Temple needed time off and Emmy couldn't do it. He wondered how Thea was doing. She would not show her feelings on the subject, but he knew she wished Carry had been closer to her. He stood in the office door and tried to imagine how the scene played out. Something must have changed when they got into the office to demand such drastic action as murder. It looked like Carry might have been near the big desk in front of the safe wall. The two overstuffed chairs and couch had not escaped the spurting blood. Carry must have been in a real temper to have her blood spurt out so fast and furious. The killer had remained calm and used a box of tissues on the desk to clean his or her shoes so they couldn't track them. The trash basket had been full of bloody tissues. They would see if it all belonged to Carry. This killer was cold blooded, that's for sure—no panic, just going about their business calmly seeing that no clue was left. "What were they doing here?" he wondered. He went back to the broken window. There was not a piece of handy cloth clinging to the glass to identify the killer. He stuck his head out the window to look at the ground. His men had covered all the bases checking for glass on the ground for signs of the window being broken from the inside. The plentiful glass on the floor under the window testified that it had indeed been broken from the outside. "Okay, no key needed for entry into the library," he said to himself. "I'll have to see if Rance survived Hillary and get started on that list. Maybe Rance used his considerable charm to get Hillary to cooperate."

Clark left the library and went back to the office to see if Rance had returned.

Five

Thea arrived at Temple's house shortly after leaving Hal. The little house was beautiful. Bruce had done a fantastic job on the house and garage. He had also built a security complex on the property at Rigby House. Since the house was on a peninsula it only needed to be guarded on one side by land and the three sea sides were now watched over by security cameras at all times. The boys were now almost fifteen months old and what little handfuls. They were toddling all over and Mrs. McMillian was wonderful at keeping them entertained when Abby was at school. At thirty-four, Abby joked that she was the oldest kid at the University of Southern Maine. She had been attending there for almost two years and would be getting her associate degree soon. She was a jewel. Thea had found her in a wash room in London as Thea was feeling ill and the friendly attendant of towels had informed Thea that she, Thea, was in the family way. Thea realized she was and had promptly hired the woman on the spot as her assistant. Neither of them had ever looked back. Mrs. McMillian was local to Rigby and Thea knew her two children from the library. They were off to college and Olivia at age forty-six was still a beautiful woman. She had raised her two sons all by herself when her husband had left her for another woman when her boys were five. It was the fact that her sons were so well behaved and adjusted that Thea first approached her to be nanny for the boys. Mrs. McMillian, as she was known to all, so the boys would respect her more, was delighted and more than glad to move into her little suite on the third floor of Rigby House.

Thea came out of her reverie to find Temple asking her to come in. Temple had made this little house a home. She had had a hard life and deserved a few breaks. She had told Thea and Emmy that her parents had thrown her out when she was seventeen because she wanted to go to college. She had pulled herself up by her bootstraps and was a very proud lady. She worked her way through college by working at the Gull every spare moment and Emmy and Thea respected her for her drive, intelligence and just plain guts. She had gotten the same degree in library science as Emmy and Thea had obtained, at the same liberal arts college, and was doing a superb job as head librarian at the Chadworth Library. She was fun and flirty and the guys all loved this beauty. She was tall and willowy with beautiful wavy black hair that she always wore up. Her eyes were a startling blue that shone out of her beautiful creamy complexion.

She asked Thea to sit down at the kitchen table and poured her a cup of tea from the pot that she had brewing on the antique black stove she had in her kitchen. Thea had given her carte blanche with the décor and she hadn't been disappointed. Temple was wonderful and patient with the children at the library and the patrons just loved her. The boys already thought she was the cat's pajamas. If Temple wasn't so proud, Thea would have already signed over the deed to the house, but she insisted on paying rent instead. Thea was collecting the rent for a down payment and would give her the full loan when she had enough. That way the house would be hers and she could be happy about the arrangement. Thea had had all she could do to convince Temple to accept the little used VW that Thea used to drive. Thea had sold it as is to her for a dollar with the warning that it might break down at any time. Thea had made sure the car was in tip top shape though. Temple didn't realize how grateful Thea was for her taking such good care of her mother's library. Mrs. Collins, the board president couldn't say enough good about her. Her assistant Webster just doted on her and he was working on his library degree too. He also worked for Henry Severied, Thea's lawyer, as a paralegal.

Thea was amazed at how calm Temple was and said so.

"Thea, I have overcome too much in my life to let Carry reach out and ruin me from the grave. I will overcome this as well. It just upsets me that she ruined our beautiful office and the library has to be closed for a few days," she said.

"The library will be put to rights as soon as we can access it. Maybe we needed to renovate anyway," said Thea. "Is it that bad, Temple?"

"I'm afraid so, Thea. It is awful. She must have been so scared."

"If it is as bad as you say I don't think she had time to be scared, Temple. Let's talk about something else for a minute. When are you coming out to see my sons? They think you are wonderful you know. You have such a way with the children."

Temple asked, "Have you heard anything from the crown about their titles yet?"

"Yes, they have approved the boys sharing the title equally. They understood that because the nurse mixed up the tags at the hospital, we had no way of knowing who was the oldest so all three will hold the title of Marquis of Tottersham. The estate will be ruled by all three with major decisions needing a majority of two for approval. I think it will work out fine. They certainly have enough assets to go around. Well, if you feel okay with being alone, I will run along to my babies," Thea said.

"Thank you, Thea. You are a good friend," Temple said.

As Thea was driving down Wheaten Street she met Andrew Vermillion going into Temple's driveway. "Uh, oh," she thought to herself.

Six

Sill Monday mid-morning

Rance Fuller had called Hillary Leighton and asked if he could have a few minutes of her time.

"You can have all the time you want, Rance," she said archly. "You know I have always had a thing for you."

Rance groaned to himself and said, "I am afraid this is official business, Hillary. I'll be right over."

He drove to the Leighton estate and wondered if he should call for back-up. Hillary was such a man-eater he wondered how the elderly butler escaped her attention. Her parents were in Europe so she would be alone and he wasn't looking forward to it. She was attractive enough, but she was a real turn-off with her mouth.

She met him at the door and ushered him into the left parlor, ordering the poor butler who had hovered near the door to bring them a drink. Rance quickly declined and said he would have to leave after asking her a few questions.

"When was the last time you saw Carry Chadworth, Hillary?" he asked.

"Now what has that girl done?" she asked. "I swear I'm not responsible for her actions you know. Sometimes I think she is not worth the effort of befriending her."

"I'm just trying to track her activities for yesterday evening if you could help me out, Hill. I know you are aware of everything that happens in your set. If you could help me it would sure go a long way with Clark."

Rance knew he was pushing her buttons with Clark. Hillary had left town after Clark had met Thea and the two of them had gotten married shortly after. She had thought that Clark was going to propose to her and she hated Thea with a passion.

"Why should I care what Clark Sanderson thinks? He has his little family now and getting bigger all the time from what I hear," she sneered.

"Now Hill, don't be like that. It doesn't become you. You are too beautiful a woman to be consumed with bitterness. Why don't you help me out and let the Lieutenant know you are being big about this?"

Hillary preened at his compliment and said, "I saw her around seven last night and she said she had found a way to get even with Thea once and for all. She was going to meet a friend and he was going to help her. He just didn't know it yet. You know how Carry could be, very secretive if she thought you might want to know what she was up to. I told her why didn't she give Thea a rest, and she laughed and said, 'Yeah, just like you do Hillary.' I told her I was tired of the whole thing and that Thea lived a charmed life anyway and nobody could hurt her. She just said 'We'll see' and went off to meet her mystery man."

"Are you really over Clark, Hill and are you going to drop your vendetta against Thea?" Rance asked.

"Sure. What's it getting me to continue? She doesn't even know I exist."

"Good girl. You don't know who this friend was she was going to meet? Have you met him before?"

"No. She said I would steal him if she introduced us so she was waiting for him to fall in love with her—like I would want her leavings, honestly Rance. Hey, what is this all about anyway?"

"Can you give me a list of her friends that you do know, Hill? It's very important," Rance asked.

"Why? Tell me Rance or I won't tell you another thing," she said.

"Hill can you tell me where you were last night between eight and midnight?" he asked.

"Why Rance? Tell me why I should answer that," she yelled.

"Hill, I was hoping I wouldn't have to break it to you this way, but Carry was murdered last night and I need to know where you were. Please tell me, Hill."

The color drained from Hillary's face and she fell back in her chair. Rance didn't think she was acting. She hadn't known that Carry was dead. She was stunned and scared at the same time.

18

"Hill, do you see why I need to know where you were and who her friends are? Help me out here. Why are you frightened, Hill? I can see that you are."

"I was here okay? All alone. What a laugh. How did she die, Rance? Please tell me. Where was she? I'll help you all I can. She was a friend such as she was."

She named a few hard cases around town and Rance thanked her and left her screaming for the butler to bring her that damned drink.

Seven

Still Monday mid-morning

Temple was still standing on the porch when Andrew pulled into her drive in his red Porsche with the top down.

"What do you want, Andrew?" she asked him.

Andrew Vermillion strode up to Temple on the porch and stood looking down at her. He was so tall that he made her feel tiny. She was not used to that feeling with most men. Andrew was a spoiled rich kid and had had everything handed to him on a platter all his life. He had always teased her about everything, not in a mean way, just in a way that irritated her. She thought he must be making fun of her because she could see no reason why he would tease her or even talk to her. She always had to wear second hand clothes and she was very conscious of their class difference. He strode up to her in kindergarten much the same way as he did just now and tweaked her hair. She had told him to leave her alone and he had asked her why. He was still asking after all these years and couldn't understand why she was so irritated every time she saw him. Andrew stood looking down at Temple and reached out and touched her hair.

"Temple, I am here to help you. Please give me a chance to say what I have to say before you give me your usual brush off," he said.

Temple backed away, she always felt so inferior and nervous when Andrew was around and she didn't like that feeling at all. Of all the men in town who flirted with her, he was the only one she couldn't respond to in a flirty way. She would bristle up at him and he would laugh, and that made her all the more angry. It had been that way for years and she was yearning that it could be different with them, but there was no way they could meet on level ground. Temple was so pragmatic that she just wouldn't accept anything but distance with Andrew. She wouldn't embarrass herself by responding to him. He was still looking down at her and she could see a soft look in his beautiful dark blue eyes that she had never seen before. He looked so much like Clark that they could be brothers instead of cousins. He had that same blonde curly hair that all the Sandersons had.

Andrew Vermillion had been given everything he could ever want in this lifetime. All he needed to do was crick his little finger and it was his. He was smart, rich, and clever and he had a thriving career as the best criminal attorney in all of Maine and beyond. Women chased him everywhere he went, but he had eyes for only one. The one he was looking at now. He had loved her from the first day he saw her in kindergarten. He had walked up to her and touched her beautiful hair. She had told him to go away and she had been telling him to go away ever since. He couldn't understand what he was doing wrong with her. She was the bravest most wonderful woman he would ever meet and he wanted her to know that, but he had never been given the chance to talk to her seriously in all the years he had known her. He had always teased her about this and that because his ego couldn't take being shot down by the woman he loved. He stood looking down into those vivid, brave blue eyes and wanted to cry. He reached out and put his hands on her arms.

"Temple, I know you are in trouble and I am going to help you. Just give me a chance. I am not teasing you or dancing anymore around the fact that I care for you. You need to accept that I am not going away. I don't know how to reach you and thaw that ice that you always put out when I am around. I have wanted to touch you and love you from the first time I ever saw you. You stood there so beautiful that you took my breath away. Even at five years old I knew there would be nobody else for me, ever. As the years went by and I saw that you were just as beautiful inside as out, my resolve became that much stronger. I don't know how to reach you, Temple. Please help me. What have I done to make you dislike me so much?"

"Andrew, I don't dislike you. I am just more practical than you are. We are from different backgrounds and anything between us could never happen. I have always steeled myself against you and it is for the best. Please don't embarrass me anymore. I am just the one who got away from you."

"My God, Temple, I will give away every cent I have if that is what is causing you to back away from me. I have never given it a thought that you would think I would look down on you, or that my family would not accept you as the wonderful person you are. You are the richest person I know. You are so self-worthy that everyone can see it at a glance. Will you at least let me help you now and can I see you socially? Please, Temple, I don't want to see you in trouble without helping you. Let's start over and pretend we are just meeting for the first time. Try to think of me as a nice person and not a rich snob, and I will think of you as the most beautiful woman I have ever met."

Temple couldn't help herself—she smiled.

Andrew gave a whoop and grabbed her in a hug. She allowed him to hug her and it felt so wonderful to finally let him touch her. She relaxed in his arms and he let out a sigh.

"I want to kiss you so bad, Temple, but I am trying not to spook you. I have waited for years and I can wait until you are ready. Now let's sit down here on your beautiful porch and you can tell me what is going on," he said.

"How did you find out about Carry? Who told you that I needed you, Andrew?" she asked.

"Clark called me and told me you were in trouble and needed a good lawyer. I was on my way before he could hang up the phone. We will get through this my darling, I promise you," he said.

Temple blushed at his term of endearment and began to tell him about her morning and what had happened on Friday in the Gull.

"Was the door to your office locked?" he asked.

"Yes, but when I went to make a sign for the front door, I saw that the lock on my office door had been jimmied with a tool, the casing was broken. I don't know how they got into the library, they must have broken a window," she said.

"Let's go to the sheriff's office so you can make your statement and we can find out a few more details. Do you want to ride with me? I will go with you in your bug if you want," he said.

"I don't mind riding in that piece of junk if you want me to go with you," she laughed as she pointed to the Porsche.

He grinned and they closed up her house and went to the sheriff's office in Andrew's "piece of junk." He couldn't believe that Temple Mathieu was finally riding with him in a car. He tried not to let her see just how worried he really was for her.

Eight

Still Monday forenoon

Clark pulled into the sheriff's office parking lot just as Rance got out of his cruiser.

Rance pretended to wipe his brow and shook his head. "The things I do for this job," he said.

Clark laughed and said, "She in rare form, was she?"

"Oh, brother was she ever! I barely escaped with my virtue. You'll be glad to know she is over you and after fresh meat," Rance laughed.

"Did she give you any names? Does she have an alibi?" Clark asked.

"She doesn't have an alibi but I would swear she didn't know Carry was dead, Clark. She went white and she also acted afraid. Why do you suppose that is? Were those two up to no good and it backfired on them? She gave me a list, and it is the usual crowd who think they have a right to a free pass in life. I don't know if we will be able to get any help from them at all but we can try."

"Let's get started. We really need to crack this in a hurry, Rance," Clark said.

They decided to work together and took Rance's vehicle. With every name on the list they asked the same questions that Rance had asked Hillary. Nobody admitted to knowing a thing and they had not seen Carry all weekend according to them. They didn't know about a mystery man or weren't talking if they did. They were all shocked to hear that Carry was dead and had been murdered. It took Clark and Rance well into the evening to go through the list. The last girl on the list, one of Hillary's special crones, did say she had seen Carry riding in an SUV earlier and that Carry had acted as if she hadn't seen her. She didn't get any particulars on the vehicle though. Maybe it was white or black. She couldn't remember. She didn't see who was driving. She didn't particularly care for Carry, she said, but she didn't kill her.

They hadn't stopped to eat lunch or supper and they were famished. A quick call to Thea got them an invite to one of Rene's yummy meals. They sat around the kitchen table discussing the case with Thea and Barry. Abby strolled in and announced that the little lords were waiting for their kiss good night from their daddy and mummy. She sat in the chair next to Barry as Thea and Clark went to say a happy goodnight to their offspring. Mrs. McMillian had them all bathed and powdered and they smelled wonderful. After a quick story they were snuggled down and sleeping in a special crib designed by their Uncle Perry so they could be together. Thea and Clark hugged tight as they looked down at their sleeping sons; they were so blessed.

Back in the kitchen they found Rance, Rene, and Barry kidding around with a very happy Abby. She was the center of their attention and was glowing. Abby hadn't had a chance to do much dating and she was having a ball flirting and laughing with all the single men in the community. She had gone to the movies several times with Rance, and Barry had taken her for dinner a few times. Rene just plain flirted with all females. Thea was pleased to see her little assistant so happy. They were all keeping it light at least for now.

They all finally remembered that Temple was in trouble and put their heads together to try and find a solution.

Abby in her typical fashion went straight to the source. "Temple is one beautiful woman with her act together. I am sure there's enough jealousy going around and plenty of people in Carry's group would want her to be in trouble. They know Temple is Thea's special friend and that would sweeten the pot. Really Thea, what is there about you that causes so much envy? I don't see that you have all that much going for you myself." Abby grinned cheekily and the guys all laughed.

They all agreed that Temple was at the heart of the killing for whatever reason and it would be tricky to learn why.

Nine

Monday forenoon
Temple's hair was blowing in the wind. She had decided she might as well remove the pins as they were all coming out anyway. Andrew almost ran off the road as he looked over and saw her beautiful wavy black hair blown by the wind in a long silky length that surprised him. He hadn't seen her with her hair down in years and he couldn't believe how long it was. He wasn't the only one who was surprised at Temple's new look. The sheriff looked at her twice and escorted them into his office for the secretary to take her statement. "You are looking mighty chipper for someone who just discovered a body, Temple," he said.

"Maybe I just discovered something else as well," she said as she looked at Andrew.

Andrew gazed at her with his heart in his eyes and it didn't take a genius to see what was happening. Sheriff Jordan was glad to see Temple finally open her eyes. Andrew stated for the record that he was Temple's attorney and she had come of her own free will to make a statement to the sheriff. Ansel Jordan made short work of her statement and told her not to leave town. He asked her if she would mind them looking through her house for bloody clothes. Andrew laughed and said, "Really, sheriff, would she be stupid enough to keep bloody clothes at her house?"

Temple said, "Here are my keys and you are welcome to search if that is okay with my attorney."

She looked at Andrew and he said, "My client has nothing to hide sheriff. We are going to lunch at the Gull if you need us for anything. Search to your heart's content."

Temple and Andrew made quite a stir when they walked into the Gull. They were smiling at each other and not quarrelling for the first time anybody ever knew. Sylvia Sanderson and Arabella Vermillion were dining at a secluded table and they both jumped to their feet and beckoned the couple over to their table. They hugged Andrew and then turned as one and hugged Temple as well.

"Oh, I am so glad to see you two finally smiling together," said Arabella. "Temple, your hair is so beautiful! Who would have guessed it would be so long and wavy. Sylvia, we simply must give a dinner so we can all get to know each other better."

"What a great idea, Bella." Sylvia said. "We will have the whole clan at my house this Saturday. I hope you don't mind having it at my house, Bella, but the triplets will be there and they just love Temple. I have all their equipment there as well. Is Saturday okay with you, Temple? We will have an informal barbeque. Then you can have the formal dinner at your place when the engagement is announced."

"Wait!" said Temple. "What engagement are you talking about?"

"Why, yours and Andrew's of course," said Arabella. "I have been waiting for this for years. Andrew has loved you forever and I want some grandbabies too," she wailed.

Andrew seeing the look on Temple's face decided to intervene. "Mother, please, will you give us a chance to sit down before you have us married off with children. We have some sad news to impart and if you will give us a second we will tell you," he said.

"Oh of course, I am sorry, Temple. Sylvia and I get carried away sometimes and think everyone else knows what we are talking about. It is just that we have known about you two for years and thought it would never happen with my stubborn son not telling you how he feels."

"Mrs. Vermillion, I am with Andrew today as his client. I am probably going to be charged with murder," Temple said in a quiet voice.

Arabella put her hand to her throat. "What nonsense, you wouldn't hurt a flea. Everyone knows you are the most kind, elegant woman in town. Who got themselves murdered, Andrew, and what are you going to do to stop this?"

Sylvia had voiced the same sentiments at the same time as her sister-in-law and the result was a gaggle of sound but Temple was grateful that they didn't consider her a suspect even without knowing the details.

Andrew quietly filled the older women in on the details of Carry's murder and they were sorry to hear of a young person's death. Neither woman cared for Carry Chadworth but they felt for Thea as her cousin. They chattered away about who would have done such a thing and then discovered they were both late for a hair appointment and hurried off after being assured that Temple would be at their barbeque on Saturday, Arabella chattering that she knew Frank would drop everything in Washington to be at Temple's party.

When they had left, a silence fell on the table where Temple and Andrew were sitting. The couple found it hard to meet each other's eyes after Arabella's blathering.

Finally Andrew cleared his throat. "Temple, please don't let mother scare you off. I don't disagree with her for a moment but I respect your reluctance to be bulldozed. I want you to be my wife and I want lots of black-haired children but we will move at your pace and not my family's; however, any time you want to jump in with plans just let me know. At the risk of being too easy, I am yours and always have been for the taking," he said.

Temple had tears in her eyes and reached out and took his hand. "Just give me some time Andrew. I had put you down in my mind as not an option and have been fighting it all my life. It will not be easy to change all at once. Now, don't you have a practice to run?"

"I will turn everything over to my assistant. You are my top priority right now. I am not working on anything else until we find Carry's killer and clear your name."

Temple's cell phone rang and Webster was on the line. "Temple, are you okay? I just found out about the murder in the library and I am so worried about you. Do you want me to come over?"

"No, Webster, I am with my attorney and we are discussing the case," she said.

"Who is your attorney? Is he any good? I can get you a good one," he said.

"My attorney is Andrew Vermillion and I understand he is the best," Temple said.

There was silence on the other end. Finally Webster said, "Isn't he the one you are always fighting with, Temple?"

"We have had a few differences of opinion but we have put that aside for the moment. I am in a precarious situation, Webster, and I need excellent legal advice right now—not to mention that Andrew is a very close friend. The library will be closed until I can get the office cleaned and refurnished. I hope you understand. I am terribly busy right now. I will call you when you can resume your duties. The library will of course continue to pay your wages while you are off."

She closed her phone and Andrew said, "My advice at the moment is to go to your house and see if the sheriff has found your bloody clothes."

She shuddered and said, "Don't even joke about it, Andrew. Someone is obviously trying to set me up and I wouldn't be surprised if they did find bloody clothes."

"Now you have me worried," he said. "Let's go."

They arrived at Temple's house as the sheriff's crew was just leaving. The sheriff met Temple and Andrew in the drive. "You have a lovely little home here, Temple, and not a sign of blood. That goes a long way toward eliminating you as a suspect."

"Thank you, Sheriff Jordan. I was just telling Andrew that I wouldn't be surprised if someone had planted evidence. They want me to take the fall obviously. I can't imagine who would hate me that much. I try not to harm anyone."

"These people are hardly reasonable, Temple. Try not to worry about it, we will find them. I will leave you in Andrew's capable hands."

The sheriff and his crew left and Temple poured them both a cup of tea she always had brewing. They sat and drank their tea and were comfortable with the silence.

"I guess I might not need a lawyer after all, Andrew. Will you be going now?" Temple asked.

"Temple, I want to be with you no matter what happens. I think I have made myself clear," he said.

He got out of his chair and went around to her. He reached down and helped her rise out of her chair. "Do you realize I have known you since we were five and I have never even kissed you? I think it is time, Temple."

He pulled her into his arms and bent his head to touch his lips lightly to hers. The world exploded into Technicolor. Temple moaned and Andrew kissed her the way he had wanted to do for years. It was a very satisfactory kiss for both of them.

Ten

Temple and Andrew spent the afternoon getting to know a little bit about each other. Andrew told her he was an only child and that his mother and father had made him work for a lot of the stuff he had as a child. They wanted him to learn responsibility. Responsibility was tops on Frank's list of structure for his son's upbringing. Coming from a long line of judges and politicians Andrew had to learn to conduct himself as a gentleman at all times. His father was well aware of the reputations of politicians and he wanted to change his little corner of the world and taught his son well. Andrew made it a practice to take on many cases *pro bono* and he was justified in having the reputation as the best criminal lawyer in the area. He didn't say that of course, but Temple knew he was the best. She had devoured every scrap of gossip about Andrew over the years, and knew he was not a womanizer. She had wondered if he was gay and told him so. He laughed and told her she was his only dream that had never been realized. He had not thought enough of any other woman to even have a serious affair. His sexual encounters were brief and uninvolved. He was up front with the few women he had dated and they either accepted that or he moved on. He was an honorable person and Temple had always known that. She just didn't think it was possible for them to connect, so she had kept her distance from him in all ways.

Temple said, "Andrew, today has been a wonderful day of pretense for me, but when you hear what I am going to tell you, that will all be over."

Temple told him she had two stepbrothers somewhere but hadn't heard from them in years. She said the last time she saw them was when she had left home at sixteen. Her mother had married Earl Scanlon and he had two sons, Jeff and Eric. Her mother had just died and her stepfather was showing all the signs that he had exhibited for years that he planned on using her for his and the boys' pleasure. She had heard them talking and she went out the bedroom window with her meager belongings in a pillow case. She left a note saying if they ever came near her again she would tell Sheriff Jordan everything. She had been working at the Gull since she was fourteen and had saved every penny she could for college. Patrick & Linda Phinney, at the Gull, had let her stay in a back room. He was a kind man and like the father she never had. She didn't tell Patrick about why she left and he never asked. He just knew she had a good reason. If he suspected anything, he never let on. He just told her if she needed help he was there. She had scraped and saved and it wasn't easy but it was all worth it. She felt she was a better person for it. Her stepfather had left the area with her two stepbrothers, Jeff and Eric, and she wouldn't know any of them if she fell over them on the sidewalk. Her brothers would be thirty-three and thirty-four now. Temple knew a lot of people in town and had come back here after college because she did know and liked a lot of people. She had spent her spare time, what little she had, with studying and talking to Thea Chadworth and Emmy Harrison. They were all from Trafton and seemed to gravitate together. Thea and Emmy were much better off than Temple but they treated her like an equal and she was pleased with their friendships. Temple had learned to feel like the luckiest person in the world for her part in the library and she was over the moon when she was chosen for head librarian by Mrs. Collins, the president of the board. She felt that Thea and Emmy had had a hand in that too. She shyly told Andrew that she had never been sexually active with anyone as her experience had left her thinking sex was a very unpleasant activity and that if he still wanted her, after knowing she was just poor white trash, he would have to accept that she was not an easy conquest. She told him she loved children but was very reluctant to bring any into this world and had decided she would enjoy other people's children instead and try to be there if she spotted any of them in trouble. She thought she knew what signs to look for. When, as a kid, she wasn't working she had spent all her time in the library to escape her home life by living in books and she loved them.

He stared at her and said, "Temple, don't ever let me hear you say you are trash again, poor or otherwise. You are the most important person in the world to me and I sure know you are not easy and anything worth having is worth waiting for." He vowed he would track those Scanlon bastards down if it was the last thing he did.

They were sitting on the couch holding hands and she put her head on his shoulder and cried. He held her tight and told her she would never be hurt again if he could help it. After a few minutes he said he should be leaving and asked her if she felt safe staying alone.

"I have been alone all my life, Andrew, and I am used to it. I have really enjoyed myself today in spite of the situation and would like to cook you a meal to make up for being such a bother," she said.

"Temple, I would not have had the courage to approach you in a serious way if you had not been in trouble. I am so grateful we had this time to get acquainted. Will you allow me to date you on a regular basis and court you in the way you should be courted?"

Temple blushed. "I think I would like that, Andrew. I have been alone too long."

He kissed her gently and left thinking to himself, "Boy if I thought it was hard before to love her at a distance, I am really going to earn my wings now."

Eleven

Tuesday morning

Sylvia visited on Tuesday to ask Thea and Clark if they thought they could make it to a barbeque on Saturday. She explained about Andrew and Temple and Thea was excited about the whole thing. Sylvia just adored her three grandsons and spent the morning sharing them with Mrs. McMillian. Abby was at school and the boys and their grandmother had a blast. Sylvia had to admit that they were little handfuls and said to be sure and invite the rest of Rigby House as well. Barry would be attending anyway as wherever the boys went Barry was not far away. Perry told Sylvia that he would help Granger with the grill and she laughed and said, "Thank God." She told Thea that actually her staff would have the meal under control but if the men wanted to feel useful with grilling the steaks they sure could. She left saying she had to tell Arabella that all was set for Saturday so she could get Frank home from Washington. She knew that Andrew would tell Temple because Arabella had said that Andrew was spending every spare moment with Temple.

Sylvia was one happy woman—her husband was now the local judge after many years in politics, she had the best son in the world, and now she had a beautiful, kind daughter-in-law and the darlingest grandbabies ever to exist. She couldn't wait for Arabella to have grandchildren, too. She hoped that Andrew and Temple would make a match of it.

A car shot out of a side street in Rigby and almost hit Sylvia's Mercedes. She swerved just in time and the dark SUV tore down the road ahead of Sylvia. Sylvia had stopped abruptly and just sat there a minute. She noticed that some comedian had named the side street "Lois Lane." She shook her head and continued on her way. She hadn't gotten a good look at the car or the driver but would mention it to Clark. She thought she glimpsed the SUV again as she came into Trafton, but couldn't be sure.

Arabella was in seventh heaven and she hugged Sylvia in a bear hug when she arrived at the Vermillion manor. "I am so happy, Syl. I think that Temple is finally giving some thought to Andrew and I couldn't be more pleased. Let's hope for the best." Sylvia told Arabella that all was set for Saturday and they clucked about what they would wear and what they would serve. They decided it was going to be a very special barbeque.

Twelve

Friday morning

Thea stood at her office window thinking. She was meeting Temple later to look over the library. Clark had told her it had been released as a crime scene. The triplets were out on the lawn with Perry and Olivia. They had seventy-seven acres to romp on and were having fun playing with a ball.

Abby was at school and all was well. Sylvia had called Clark and told him about the SUV almost hitting her and Clark said he would keep an eye out for it. Thea was glad Sylvia hadn't been hit. She loved her mother-in-law and the triplets adored her. Of course they loved everyone. She went outside and helped them catch the ball. She had to leave in an hour to meet Temple. She was so glad she had all these people to help her with her babies. She didn't worry about leaving them anymore.

Thea met Temple at the library and she was glowing. She told Thea she was more at ease with Andrew and had told him everything about her life. She also told Thea the truth about why she had left home so young. Thea hugged her and said. "Oh, Temple, Emmy and I would never have thought any less of you because you were the victim of those monsters you lived with. Let me know if you want to talk about it at any time. I can't believe how much you have suffered. Do you think they might want to hurt you now?" she asked Temple.

"I don't see why they would after all these years. I'm sure they have forgotten all about me by now. God knows I want to forget them," she said.

They entered the library together and approached the office with trepidation. Thea had hired a crime scene cleanup crew to clean up the blood. It wasn't too bad—just an empty room with a safe on the wall.

"I told them to remove everything with blood on it and I guess they did. I told them to save any paperwork for you to go over and then you can trash it. I am sorry you have to handle that stuff."

"It has to be done, Thea. Let's make plans."

They had brought sketch pads and went to work designing a new room. The broken window had been replaced at the behest of Clark and a new lock had been put on the door. Barry had stopped by to pick up the shadow box and artifacts and was making sure they were thoroughly cleaned. Thea had asked Bruce to stop by and he arrived as they were finishing their sketches. They explained what they wanted and he said he would get Emmy to handle everything. They left it in Emmy's hands and agreed that the rest of the library could use a good redo and Emmy was called over for a consult.

Emmy arrived a half hour later with sandwiches and sodas for everyone and they set to discussing a whole new theme for the library. Andrea Collins was called and informed of their plans and she couldn't agree more that a new image was needed to make people forget what had happened there. Temple and Emmy said they would keep Thea informed and she could drop in at any time to see their progress. Thea left them happily making plans and ordering supplies. Thea had given them carte blanche to do anything they wanted and it wouldn't be cheap; she knew Emmy.

Thirteen

Friday afternoon

Clark had listened to his mother tell him about the dark SUV and he dismissed it as a reckless driver. He would keep an eye out for it though. His mother could have been hurt. They had finished with any evidence at the library and closed out the crime scene. The girls were busy remodeling. He thought it was a good idea; the town needed a complete change to want to go into the library now. He was glad that Ansel had cleared Temple tentatively as a suspect. She had enough on her plate. Thea had told him and Barry about what Temple had told her and Andrew. Temple had said she didn't care if Thea told Clark and Barry because now that she had talked about it she felt free once and for all. Andrew had already been in touch with Clark and they were trying to trace the Scanlons to find out where they were. They were being circumspect so they wouldn't draw attention to Temple if they lived far away from Trafton. Let sleeping dogs lie, as Temple had escaped in time—they really couldn't charge them with anything. Barry had told Clark that he had been working at the Gull at the time and he knew that Temple had left her home for a good reason and suspected what it might be as he knew her stepbrothers. He paid them a visit and let them know that any moves they made toward Temple would be met with a reckoning from him. Clark smiled to think of the big security master confronting those three animals.

They would just be sure there were no female children in the Scanlons' care when they caught up with them. Clark would have to keep Andrew from breaking a few heads though. When it came to Temple he was a wild man.

Clark and his crew continued to interview Carry's friends, hoping somebody would remember something or crack on something they did know. Hillary continued to act frightened but would not admit to it and got very surly when she was pushed.

"Either charge me or leave me alone," she screamed at Rance on his third visit.

The girl who had seen Carry in an SUV remembered that it was dark in color. She was sure that it was dark because she remembered that Carry's white face stood out against it. Whether it was hindsight or drama was hard to tell. They would just have to keep plugging away.

Clark asked Rance if he would like to come to the Saturday shindig and he said he would be there just to see Abby. Ansel Jordan and his wife Ruby were invited as well.

Clark and Barry had gone over to the library and set it up for a state of the art alarm system and Barry's security company would install it on Monday. Thea had asked him to put a security system in Temple's house as well and that was already installed. Barry's crew had done it yesterday. Thea had a way of getting things done in a hurry, and she was worried about Temple—not that she was spending much time alone Barry thought and chuckled. He decided to get the everyday business out of the way so his team and the sheriff could enjoy themselves tomorrow.

Clark went to talk with Wanda and Hal Chadworth to see if they knew anyone who had threatened Carry. Tony was there too and he wanted to speak to Clark alone so they stepped out onto the porch.

"I think Carry was seeing someone from out of town," he said.

"What makes you think that, Tony?" Clark asked. "Did she say anything to you about it?"

"No, but she took the phone bill when it came in and paid it herself. Believe me that is not like Carry to part with any of her money if she could get Dad to pay it for her. She has been acting more sneaky than usual, too," Tony said. "She also destroyed the bill after she paid it. How weird is that?"

"I'd say she was hiding something all right. We checked her cell for any strange calls but didn't think she would call from the home landline. I'll have to ask your dad's permission to check his bill. Is there anything else that comes to mind, Tony?" Clark asked.

"She was always looking over her shoulder, so to speak, for the last couple of weeks. If there was any loud noise she would jump a mile. I am dating Shelly Parker and even she noticed that Carry was acting spooky. I think Carry crossed the wrong person, Clark. She hated Thea with a passion especially after Dad took Thea's side about the arson on Thea's house. Her hate extended over to Temple because Thea and Temple were such chums. I shudder to think what Carry could have come up with to cause them trouble. She might have looked for help in hurting them with someone they knew. I just thought you would need to know these things," Tony said.

"Thanks, Tony, that gives me a few ideas. I appreciate your help," Clark said.

Clark got permission from Hal to look at his records and left after finding that neither Hall nor Wanda could think of anyone in particular that had it in for Carry. She had been acting secretive lately but other than that they couldn't help him.

Clark got Rance busy on checking phone records and decided to talk with Hillary himself.

Hillary greeted him coolly when the butler showed him in and told him she had answered all the questions she was going to.

"If you are not here for some decent sex, Clark, don't bother me," she sneered.

"Hillary, we are slowly uncovering an angle that Carry was taking and I think you know something about it. You can see where it got her and if whoever killed her thinks that you know anything you would do well to help us. Your chintzy veneer is slipping and I think you want to live. Tell me what you know or I will tell your father you need a body guard. I don't think you want him to know you are still up to no good when it comes to Thea and Temple," Clark threatened.

"All I know is that she told me she was finally going to hurt Thea. She thought that I would be interested, but I told her to leave me out of it. I couldn't care less about your stinking bride and her lowlife friends so do your worst, Clark," she screamed.

Clark looked at Hillary and said, "As far as you are concerned, Hillary, I intend to do nothing. If you are harmed, let it be on your own head. I will show myself out."

An ashtray hit the salon door as Clark closed it and he left quietly after raising a hand to the butler hovering in the hall.

Fourteen

Sylvia and Granger Sanderson hadn't had a shindig like this in a long time. Arabella had arrived early and she and Sylvia had been right out straight ever since. It seemed like half the town was coming and they wanted it to be fun for all. Sylvia had asked Barry for extra security for screening guests to be sure nobody that was not wanted showed up; her own security people on the gate had that covered as well. She wanted to be sure that the babies could play without worry. The guests began arriving at ten o'clock and drinks and hors d'oeuvres were available everywhere.

Clark and his entourage arrived with great fanfare and everyone rushed to play with the boys. Temple and Andrew arrived shortly after and the boys all streaked to Temple and wanted to be picked up. Between the two of them, Andrew and Temple scooped the three of them up and they squealed with delight. Thea laughed and said, "Of course those poor babies haven't had any attention today."

Temple was overwhelmed with the people that had come. They all crowded around her and Andrew to say how glad they were to see them together.

Abby had arrived with Barry and Mrs. McMillian and Rance made a bee line for her. Her time was taken up however with helping Mrs. McMillian and Thea feed the boys and seeing that they had a good time. There would be plenty of time for socializing when the boys went down for their nap. In the meantime the triplets toddled all over the place and had a great time with all the oohs and aahs that they got from everyone. The three little blond toddlers were the hit of the party and exhausted themselves in short order. Perry and Mrs. McMillian designated themselves to put the boys down for their naps and they departed to the special room that Sylvia and Granger had set up for when the boys visited.

Abby had a ball with all the single men vying for her attention. Music was playing and the stone-floored patio was cleared for dancing and everyone was enjoying themselves.

Sylvia asked Thea if she thought that Hal and Wanda would be upset with the frivolities so soon after Carry's death.

"I don't think Uncle Hal would give it a thought. He doesn't exactly party that much anyway. Carry's body is not going to be released until next week sometime and they are keeping close to home. I would have liked him to be here to see the triplets but we will go see them soon," Thea said.

Ansel and Ruby Jordan were chatting with Arabella and Frank Vermillion when Ansel's phone rang. It was dispatch and Clark and Barry got a similar call. The security system had detected someone on the premises at Temple's house on Wheaten Street and a car was on the way. The sheriff's team of Clark, Rance, and the sheriff left in a hurry and Barry was already on the way. Temple and Andrew decided to wait for word and remained at the Sandersons', worrying.

The others made an attempt to take their minds off what was happening and they were surrounded by friends. Patrick and Linda Phinney were there to support them as well as Abby and her stable of fellows. Temple was really beautiful today with her black wavy hair worn down with the front loosely caught up in a barrette. Her bright blue eyes were sparkling and so was Andrew. They tried to pretend that all was well. Temple had on a blue sundress that matched her eyes perfectly and Abby said it was too bad that Andrew had to settle for such an ugly duckling. Everyone laughed and some of the tension left the group. Leave it to Abby to lighten things up, thought Thea.

Abby and Thea also had their hair down and Emmy remarked as she came up to the group with Bruce, "I don't know why I didn't get the memo to wear my hair down." She had her own dark hair caught up in a ponytail and looked adorable in a lime green sun suit. Thea was wearing a white eyelet lace sundress and her long dark auburn hair flowed down her back in a bright rain of waves. Abby was gorgeous in a bright pink peasant blouse and skirt. Her long blond curls cascaded down her back and she had just left them wild and free. Her soft brown eyes were happy as she looked around at her adopted family and friends. Abby was a favorite with everybody and Thea was so glad she had found her.

The food was sensational and Frank campaigned unashamedly and Arabella bubbled over. She was so happy that Temple and Andrew were together and Frank was pleased as well.

The sheriff's crowd came back and explained that someone had tried to open Temple's front door and the alarm must have frightened them off. Clark was not gentle with telling Temple that he didn't want her staying alone in the house at the end of the cul-de-sac. Andrew seconded the motion and Temple agreed to allow a security guard stationed at her door for a while.

After the guys that had left had a chance to eat and socialize for a few hours, the party began to break up. The babies woke up and were playing with their toys while a smiling Perry and a flushed Mrs. McMillian had a meal before the Rigby House crowd packed up and headed for home.

Thea couldn't help notice that Perry and Mrs. McMillian had grown a little closer this afternoon. She hoped that Uncle Perry would find some happiness with Olivia. They both deserved it.

Temple and Andrew looked so happy together as they left the Sanderson house. Thea wished them nothing but joy. They were headed back to Temple's house and then Barry was going to arrange for some extra security for her.

Andrew pulled his Porsche into the drive and walked Temple to the door. After a long slow goodbye kiss he said he would be back in a little while. Temple watched him drive away and sighed with happiness. She couldn't believe how happy she was. Andrew was the real deal and she knew it. She would tell him the next time she saw him that she would marry him.

Fifteen

Six o'clock Saturday afternoon

Temple had her little house spotless and she was dressed casually in a nice pair of jeans and a warm pink sweater. She looked in the mirror and thought she had never looked happier. She and Andrew were going to go walking on the shore tonight. It would be the most romantic night of her life.

Temple remembered that she had to get the library designs out of her little VW and she turned off the alarm to the garage and went out to get them. She turned the corner by the house to go to her unattached garage when everything went black.

Andrew pulled into the drive of Temple's house on Wheaten Street and went to the door of the house. He was a little late because he had stopped at his mother's to get the heirloom ring that all the Vermillion men had given to their prospective brides. He was going to ask Temple to marry him again and he was hoping for a yes this time. He knocked on the door and waited for her to answer. He kept knocking and she didn't answer. He went around to the side where the garage was and noticed blood on the ground by the corner of the house. Andrew's heart stopped. He raced to the garage and found it still locked. He ran back to the house and pounded on the door. This time when Temple didn't answer he tried the door and it was locked too. He pulled out his cell and called the sheriff's department. He then called Clark and told him he was going to break down the door.

"Wait, Andrew," Clark said. "She might just be in the shower or ran to the store for something. Is there a lot of blood?"

"No, just enough to be noticeable," Andrew said "I hope she didn't cut herself or something. She was going to fix us a nice supper."

"We're on our way. Stay calm and wait for us to get there Thea has a key and we can check the house," Clark said.

Andrew spent the longest ten minutes of his life waiting for Rance to arrive at Temple's house. The sheriff wasn't far behind and they began a search of the property. It was hard to tell if a car had been there other than Temple's and Andrew's because of the activity earlier when the guys had checked the premises after the alarm had gone off. They had just stepped out of the woods when Clark and Thea arrived from Rigby House in a record eighteen minutes with siren and lights blaring all the way. Barry was right behind them. They all jumped out of their vehicles and raced to the door. Thea opened the door and no alarm sounded. The house was immaculate. No sign of cooking in the kitchen and no sign that Temple had started any preparation for a meal. There was a crudely written note on the table.

It read:

ok rich man. I saw you kiss her. she is mine now. if you want her back unharmed it will cost you. Put 3 million dolors in a suitcase and wait for my call. i mean busniss. if i see a cop she is histry.

Andrew let out the worst noise that Thea had ever heard. It sounded like he was caught in a bear trap. Clark took the note in gloved hands and started to give orders. They opened the garage and her little car was still there. Thea pulled on a pair of gloves and began checking for Temple's purse and money without touching anything else. They were all there.

She looked at Clark and said, "If this is about money, why didn't he take her purse and money? I don't like this, Clark. Something isn't right about this and that note is fishy, too."

"I know, darling. We will find her. Think, Thea. Did she ever mention anyone that might have wanted to date her or something and she turned them down?" Clark said.

"Every red-blooded male in Trafton wanted to date Temple, but she just laughed and flirted back with them and they all took it in stride. They knew she was not serious and she never led anyone on either," Thea said.

Andrew had rushed out the door and called his father to get the money ready as soon as possible. He knew it was hopeless to think it would protect Temple's life to get the money, but it gave him something to do. He was a criminal attorney; he knew how these things turned out. He had to have faith in Clark and his team to find her. He was a desperate man.

Clark had his team searching every nook and cranny for fingerprints and evidence. They canvassed the neighborhood asking if anyone had seen anything suspicious. Nobody had noticed anything—they were all in their back yards having barbeques. They had lost interest after the cops had all screeched up earlier in the day. One woman had seen a dark SUV before that but it didn't stay at the end of the street very long. It had left before the cops had arrived earlier. She didn't notice anything about the driver. The windows were all dark. She had come back to her kitchen for ice a little while ago and thought she had seen the same vehicle again but didn't pay attention.

Clark put out a stop on all dark SUVs. That would only make it a little million to check. He wondered what connection this might be to the killing at the library.

Emmy and Bruce had arrived and wanted to know what they could do. Clark told them they all had to wait for the phone call. Andrew had come back into the house and was sitting right on top of the phone. Frank would have the money in a couple of hours and they needed to wait for instructions. Clark had two helicopters on standby to try and keep track of the kidnapper when he called. They all knew it didn't look good for Temple and nobody was optimistic. Barry put his men on double alert at Rigby House in case this was a plot to distract Thea and Clark.

Thea and Clark had taken special classes on kidnapping to avert any danger to the little lords and they knew what to expect from a kidnapper. It was not in the kidnapper's best interest to keep the victim alive. They were both heartsick for Andrew and Temple. Everyone was praying for Temple to be all right.

Sixteen

Nine o'clock Saturday night

Temple's head felt like it was going to explode. She had already thrown up as soon as she became conscious. The vomit had just come up and she was covered with it. She reeked and felt like she was going to be sick again. She was in a sitting position against a wall on a dirty bed. She knew it was dirty because she could smell it even over the vomit. It was pitch dark and her hands and feet were tied. She was so glad they had not put a gag on her. She would have choked to death on her own vomit. She could hear voices but thought it was a TV in another room. Her hair felt matted and she knew it was from dried blood. "That was good. Wasn't it?" She didn't know. She thought the wound had stopped bleeding. She wished her head would stop aching. She was sick again and more discomfort was added to her already bad situation. She apparently had lost control of her bodily functions and her pants were soaking with urine and God knows what else. "Would they kill her? Would they rape her?" She was glad she was a mess. She had read that if you were attacked and could force yourself to pee and poop the attacker would get so disgusted that he wouldn't rape you. She felt she fit that category by now. "What would Andrew think? Would he look for her?" She was so standoffish sometimes he might think she changed her mind about him and go home. She was so tired. She needed to think. The tethers on her hands were so tight she could hardly feel her fingers. She shifted position and lay down on the dirty bed with her hands against her wet pants, blessed sleep overtook her.

Seventeen

Nine Thirty Saturday Night/ the killer

   The door opened and a man looked cautiously into the room. He had a mask over his head in case she was awake. She was asleep. God she was a mess and she stunk to high heaven. How could he have ever thought she was the sexiest woman alive? He would take the money and run. He had thought that if he had enough money she might agree to go with him, but he didn't want her now. She was sullied in his eyes. She had kissed that lawyer pig and look at her now. Gone was his goddess and in her place was this mass of stink. He didn't even want to get close enough to kill her. No matter, nobody would ever find her for months. This dump was so deserted it had been perfect for his purposes. He had to get the money from those rich bastards and then he would be gone. Maybe he shouldn't have slit the bitch's throat but she made him mad. When she dissed Temple like that he saw red and grabbed the knife. He really had to watch his temper. He had hit Temple a little too hard because she had kissed that damned lawyer. Maybe that bitch Carry would have run away with him; she had delusions of grandeur, that's for sure, and she sure could screw. Too late now, they would never catch him, they would never suspect him in a million years. Carry was right about money being everything. She had talked him into breaking into the library with the promise of riches just to find out that all that was in the safe was some damned manuscripts that belonged to Thea's mother. Carry had been insane in her hatred of Thea and Temple. He just lost it when she called Temple that awful name and now the Temple he knew and loved is dead. Oh, well. "It's time to make the call; so long, goddess, ha ha."

Eighteen

Two o'clock Sunday morning

Except for the man on the phone tap Clark and the rest had left to look for the SUV and try to get more information on the kidnapper. Andrew sat at the kitchen table with his head in his hands. The money was in a large suitcase of Arabella's packed tightly and secure by his side. He was waiting for the call to come in. Thea was with him and they were saturated with coffee by now.

The phone rang. Andrew grabbed it and said, "Hello."

A garbled voice said "Do you have the money with you?"

"Yes, for God's sake don't hurt her. I'll do whatever you want."

"Good. Now listen carefully because your honey's life depends on it. I want you to get in that fancy car of yours and drive to Elliott Wharf. I want you to go to the end of the wharf and set the suitcase right on the edge of the pier. You have just ten minutes to get there and set it down. You are being watched and if any cops show up dear Temple is no more. Do you understand my orders?" the voice said.

"Yes. I am on my way. How will I know where to find Temple?" Andrew said.

"If you do exactly as I said you will have her inside of an hour. Set the suitcase down and leave the pier immediately. Don't look back and no cops. I mean business, fella," the kidnapper said and hung up.

Andrew scrambled for his car with the heavy suitcase and threw it in the back. Thea jumped in beside him and he tore out of the drive. They didn't even wait to see if they got a fix on the caller. Elliott Wharf was just ten minutes away and they couldn't spare a second. The wharf was on the road to Rigby and Andrew knew it well. It went way out into the Atlantic and this time of the morning it would be deserted. The Porsche got them there on time and Andrew told Thea to stay out of sight. He grabbed the suitcase and raced out onto the pier. He set it right on the edge and turned around and raced back to his car. He left in a cloud of dust to get back to the phone.

Clark had gotten the call from Rance who didn't have a chance to get a fix on the caller. He alerted Clark to the situation and Clark put the copters in the air. He warned them to be discreet but knew it would be too late to get the kidnapper. They were dealing with a wily mind.

Nineteen

Two fourteen Sunday morning/ the killer

The suitcase suddenly disappeared from the end of the pier and all was pitch dark. The kidnapper was in the water in full scuba gear and had tied a line to the suitcase. The suitcase was very expensive and water tight. The kidnapper played out his line and swam for the opposite cove. The suitcase bobbed happily along at the end of the line and was invisible to anyone watching. If they could see it they would see it moving steadily towards the little cove several hundred feet away. He heard the copters overhead as he came out of the water but he was well hidden. Lights from the copter played along the beach and water but his car was hidden in a little shack. He grabbed the suitcase and dumped its contents into a large box in his car. He then tossed the suitcase back into the water after checking for bugs on the money and jumped into his SUV and sped out of the cove with his lights out. He knew the way with his eyes closed. In ten minutes he was in his garage with the door down and nobody the wiser. He threw his head back and laughed until he cried. He went into the house through the garage and tossed the box on his couch. The whole operation had taken less than thirty minutes and he was home free. He hoped that the fancy lawyer would have a fun time waiting for the call that would never come. He giggled again to himself and took off his gloves and wet suit and tossed the money in the air. They had actually given him all the money from what he could tell and he thought "suckers."

Twenty

Four o'clock Sunday morning

Andrew was pacing the floor and he knew that the kidnapper was not going to call. He was inconsolable and Thea didn't even try to make him feel better. She just sat quietly and supported him with her presence. The babies were long in bed and Clark was tearing his hair at being outfoxed by the damn kidnapper. He had finally checked his desk for any info on Temple's stepfamily and found a few surprises that would have helped earlier maybe. Her stepfather, Earl Scanlon, was dead. He had been killed in a car accident and the boys had come into a small windfall and purchased an underwater scuba diving business last year that just so happened to be in Bar Harbor, Maine. Clark threw the paper across the room. It might have helped but he doubted it. These guys were clever. How would they be able to find Temple? He launched an inquiry with the Bar Harbor police and they said they would check out the Scanlon brothers and their business to see if they were out of town and maybe have Temple on the premises. Temple had been missing now for over ten hours as far as they knew and she was hurt. He alerted the EMTs at the station to be on standby and he went out to join his men in the manhunt.

Andrew's cell phone rang and he jumped out of his skin. He answered with a sharp "Hello." And Sylvia apologized for scaring him. She said she couldn't get that dark SUV that had almost hit her out of her mind and wondered if it could be connected with the kidnapping. She hadn't wanted to bother Clark as he had been on the phone with another police department on a lead according to the dispatcher.

"What are you talking about, Aunt Sylvia?" Andrew asked. "An SUV almost hit you when?"

Thea's head snapped up and she waved for Andrew's attention that she knew about it. Sylvia continued to tell Andrew where the car had almost hit her and she just wanted him to check the area.

Andrew, desperate for something to do, said he would go take a look. Thea said she would go with him as two sets of eyes were better than one. As they climbed into the Porsche, Andrew's cell rang again.

Twenty-One

Three o'clock Sunday morning

Temple's head wasn't aching as bad when she woke the second time. Everything rushed back at her as the terrible stench overpowered her once again. How she could have slept through that she didn't know. Her arm sockets were aching from being behind her and her left hip was very sore for some reason. Maybe they had hit her there. As she shifted position she felt the reason for the ache in her hip. Her cell phone! She had put it in her jeans pocket when she changed and apparently the kidnappers had not checked her pockets. If she could just get her hands free. She began to worry at the bonds and to her surprise remembered that her fingers were numb when she fell asleep, now they were just sore. The bonds were very slippery because her hands had been under her wet pants for hours. She couldn't see what material tied her feet because of the dark but it felt like rawhide on her hands. Very slippery rawhide. She remembered that Barry had shown her some that they made moccasins out of and had explained that it got very slippery when it was wet. If you used wet rawhide on things like snowshoes and such, it would be very tight when it dried. It stood to reason that if the kidnapper had used dry rawhide to bind her hands then when it got wet it would stretch a little. She began to work furiously pulling and stretching the rawhide on her hands. She knew the liquid that had wet the bindings was not appetizing but if she could get free it would be worth it. She hoped the kidnappers would not come back too soon. She was able to loosen the ties a little and she frantically kept at it until she finally was able to slip her sore miserable hands free of her bonds. As soon as she rested her hands a minute she started in on her feet and soon had them free also. She reached into her pocket and pulled out her phone. Light, beautiful light. Her phone allowed her to scan the room for windows but she found none and the door was barred from the other side. She hit speed dial for Andrew and he answered on the first ring.

"Hello," Andrew said.

"Andrew, please help me. I've been kidnapped and I think they are going to kill me," Temple cried.

"Where are you darling? We will come and get you," Andrew said. "I am so glad you are alive."

"I don't know for how long, Andrew, and I don't know where I am. I am locked in a filthy room with no windows and the door is barred. I am a mess. I don't want you to see me like this. I was sick all over myself and when I was unconscious, I lost control of myself and I stink," she wailed.

"Darling, listen. Can you hear anything to give you some idea where you are? Are you near water? Railroad tracks?" he asked.

"I don't think so," she answered.

"Darling I have Thea with me and she is on her phone with Clark. We have been looking all over for you. Thea and I are following a clue that Sylvia gave us. I will call you back in ten minutes; you need to save your battery. I love you, Temple."

"I love you too Andrew," she said.

Thea saw Andrew light up like a Christmas tree and she knew what Temple had said. She told Clark where they were headed and he said it was a good idea and he would begin to mosey in that direction.

They slowed down when they got to Lois Lane and Andrew made the turn into the lane. It had nice houses in a small development and they drove slowly looking for clues. Way down at the end of the development was an old farmhouse that had been abandoned when the land was sold to the developer. In the headlights there appeared to be trampled grass near the house. Andrew picked up his phone and hit Temple's speed dial. She answered on the first ring and Andrew drew a deep breath.

"Listen, my darling, and tell me what you hear," he said.

He then laid his hand on the Porsche's horn and kept it there until he heard Temple say, "I hear the horn on that old piece of junk you drive, my darling."

Andrew grabbed a flashlight and kept the lights of the Porsche trained on the front door. "Thea, please call an ambulance and get Clark over here." He then grabbed a blanket from the trunk and rushed into the old farmhouse. He didn't stop to think that the kidnapper could be in there; he didn't care. He would tear them limb from limb.

"Temple, where are you?" he shouted.

He heard a small squeak over his head and followed the sound to a small box room in the attic. The door was barred and he could hear Temple crying on the other side. He ripped the bar off the door and wrenched the door open. She was standing in the middle of the small room trying to hide from him. She was crying with humiliation and Andrew rushed over to her and threw the blanket around her. Then he scooped her up in his arms and rushed from the God-forsaken house. The EMTs that Clark had on standby were just screaming up the road in their ambulance. Andrew put his foot on the back bumper and set Temple on his thigh so the attendant could look at her head. They checked her head and eyes and said she probably had a concussion and needed to go to the hospital. Temple turned to Andrew and shrunk down in a ball. "Can she have a shower and some food before she comes in? I will be gentle with her but she needs nourishment more than anything right now and I will bring her in myself in an hour or so," he said.

"Just be sure you get her there as soon as you can and be careful of her head wound. It is small but deep and she needs treatment for her concussion."

"I promise I will take good care of her," Andrew said as he put Temple in the passenger seat of the Porsche. Temple started to protest that she was dirty and he kissed her right on the mouth in front of God and everyone.

Thea had climbed into the back compartment and said, "We are closer to Rigby House, Temple, and you can clean up there."

Temple looked at Andrew and he read her mind. "She is going to go to her own house, Thea, and I will see that she gets all the attention she needs."

Thea said, "I understand."

They met Clark and two other sheriffs' cars at the turn to Lois Lane. Thea jumped out and said, "I will show them where to go, Andrew, and leave Temple to you."

Twenty-Two

Early Sunday Morning

Andrew turned toward Trafton and drove very sedately for him until they arrived at the little house on Wheaten Road. Temple started to get out of the car and Andrew said, "I will do it my darling; a shower first and then a long bath while I bring you some food and something to drink." He went ahead and opened the door and then he came back for Temple. He picked her up and dropped her blanket on the porch as they reached the door. He then peeled her jeans and sweater from her tired body and picked her up again. He carried her to the bathroom and turned on the shower full force being careful to shampoo her head very carefully. The cut oozed just a little and he was reassured that she might just be all right. He knew she was embarrassed about her smell and decided to make a joke of it. "After we get you hosed off," he joked, "we will drop you into a nice scented bath and you will be as good as new."

She laughed and punched him feebly. "You will probably have to burn the Porsche. I don't think you will get the smell out, Andrew."

"Oh well, the things I have to do for my woman," he laughed.

He soaped her all over and while she was rinsing he drew a nice warm bath and put her scent in it. She wasn't embarrassed that he was seeing her naked and he had joked away her humiliation. She was so grateful for him. He put her in the bath and went to get her a meal and something cold to drink. He brought her iced lemonade that Thea had fixed and a couple of the sandwiches that Thea had brought in for the crew while waiting for the call. She was ravenous and sighed when she was done.

"Do I have to go to the hospital?" she asked. "I feel so good right here."

"Unless you want half the town pounding on the door, we have to, my love." He said, "I don't want anything else to happen to you, Temple, and I will be staying right by your side, smelly or sweet, and hope you want me to. Will you marry me, darling?"

"Are you sure you want to marry me now that you've seen me at my worst?" she asked.

"As far as I am concerned, Temple, when I saw you standing there in all your glory, you were the most beautiful sight in the world. I love you now and forever."

"I love you too, Andrew, and I will marry you."

Andrew whooped and scooped her out of the tub. "You will look like a prune if you stay in any longer and we need to get you to the hospital. I would rather delay a little and consummate our love but a promise is a promise and you will be staying in the hospital tonight unless I miss my guess."

He set her on the bed and said in a strangled voice, "Temple, you are the most beautiful woman in the world. Can you dress yourself? I don't trust myself with you any longer."

She laughed and he left the room and used a little cleaner on the seat of his car while she dressed. He had sponged his own clothes off when he was in the bathroom and all was fine. He gathered up her soiled clothes and bagged them for the rubbish and put them in the garage. When Temple was ready he set the alarm and took her to the hospital.

It was eight o'clock in the morning by the time she was admitted and with the tests that had to be done she was told she needed to stay at least for one night. Andrew determined to stay by her side and Clark put a guard outside her door. Thea and Emmy shopped and cleaned Temple's house so she would have no reminders of the wait that took place while she was gone.

Arabella was the first to know (except Thea) that there would indeed be a wedding very soon. As Andrew had put it, "Mother, make it fast. I can't wait."

Arabella and Sylvia went into high gear.

Twenty-Three

Three weeks later

Clark was frustrated. He had been bested by the kidnapper and he was trying to get some clue as to who it was. He was convinced the kidnapper and Carry's killer were one and the same person or persons. Temple had not been able to tell him anything and there were no usable prints in the old farmhouse. Temple had been unconscious and didn't know how many kidnappers there were.

Clark was totally in charge of the investigation and was casting his line in many different directions. The Bar Harbor police had reported that both Scanlon brothers were at home when they found them at about nine o'clock Sunday morning which only proved they had ample time to pull everything off and the expertise to do it. From all reports from Bar Harbor, the brothers were respectable businessmen and their business seemed to be doing well. They were both in long-term relationships with no children involved at all. He was now checking on other sources in the expertise department.

Clark pulled into the drive of a small dock and boating outfit. The owner was Sylvia's cousin on her mother's side and was a salty old gent; a true down-easter. Clark knew that Peter "Happy" Sturgis was a fountain of knowledge to everything that happened in the area. He found him scraping the bottom of a small rental boat that he had upturned on a platform. He made a decent living renting boats and fishing equipment to tourists and they loved his old salt attitude. It was not put on for their benefit—it was truly just the way Hap was. His Maine accent thrilled the tourists and if he cared what they thought he would probably be offended. When he was ill a few years ago, Sylvia had tried to lend him some money. He quickly informed her he could row his own boat and didn't need any help from others.

Hap greeted Clark with a big grin. "Been a while, son," he said. "I haven't seen you since you grabbed up that nice little Thea

Chadworth. I hear you are the proud daddy of triplets. Always knew you were an over achiever. Ha ha ha."

Clark grinned at his old cousin and shook his hand. Hap was one of his biggest supporters and told everyone he knew about his smart relative. When Clark had decided to become a deputy sheriff Hap knew it was the perfect job for him. He had advised the young squirt since he was knee high to a grasshopper.

"What you got up your sleeve now, Clark?" he asked. "I suppose you are looking into that kidnapping of little Temple Mathieu?"

"Well, I wondered if you had any ideas, Hap? I am at a standstill right now. I am checking the scuba divers in the area and thought you might be able to steer me in the right direction," Clark said.

"Awful lot of them tourists bring their own gear. Hard to pin that angle down son. I'll keep my ears open though. Folks can't help brag about outwitting the cops you know. How is that little girl anyway? She sure has had a rough life. Hear ole Andrew has finally got a yes from her, huh? She is fine as kine with all that gypsy hair. Quite a beauty. Looks like her ma did at that age. I kind of had a crush on her, Temple's ma that is, but she only had eyes for Scanlon. Sherri Murphy Mathieu was a beauty and she knew it. She was running around with Scanlon while she was married to Templeton Mathieu and Templeton adored his family. One day he just went out in his lobster boat and the boat went down; they never found his body. You win some you lose some. Temple is going to break a lot of hearts getting married. I reckon there isn't a fellow in all of Trafton that hasn't fantasized about marrying her."

Hap Sturgis is one of the few people in down-east Maine who really knows the true descriptive phrase of "finest kind." The out-of-state tourists had heard the down-east native say "fine as kine" to identify a particularly nice subject and had heard it as finest kind. They ran with the phrase and the old timers laughed among themselves about the wrong usage. They would never correct them. "Let 'em make fools of themselves," they thought. Now the true phrase was all but forgotten except by a few old-timers like Hap. Even the natives accepted the new phrase, many not knowing the difference themselves. Their parents and elders had not bothered to correct them either. Kine were particularly fine-haired cattle that early down-east farmers had run on their farms, thus the saying.

Clark thanked Hap and said he would have to come see those sturdy little cousins of his and he was on his way knowing that Hap would be on the lookout for anything of interest to him.

Clark stopped at the library where there was a bustle of activity. Bruce and Emmy had outdone themselves on the office. It was really magnificent. Thea and Temple were sitting on a beautiful light beige leather couch that matched two comfy chairs. The new desk was in itself a masterpiece. It was oak and truly beautiful. A matching desk chair of beige leather was filled with Emmy's delighted rump. They were chatting a mile a minute and reveling in the beauty of their surroundings. The solid oak floor had been sanded and polished to within an inch of its life and was covered with an original Turkey carpet. The bright colors in the carpet were picked up in the handsome drapes at the window to alter the effect of the beautiful oak paneling on the walls. The whole was a bright happy room. Emmy couldn't have chosen a better color scheme to make the viewer forget a vicious murder had taken place in this room. The library was built so that the office window was actually on the second floor and the view was as splendid as the office. It overlooked a garden that the girls had taken particular pains with and the flowers were beautiful. Clark noticed that they had poor Webster mowing the grass and he chuckled. Temple, noticing the direction of his glance, said, "Webster wanted to earn the money that the library has been paying him while we are closed and he is doing wonders with the lawn. He is also helping us transfer all the books from one area to another. He will be a tremendous help when I go on my honeymoon. Thea and Emmy will cover for me while I am gone."

Clark had noticed that the front desk and surround had been transformed into a neat place to do business and everywhere bright and cheery was the theme. The brand new oak stacks had been modified with sturdy ceiling tracks that made them glide like silk and enable three rows to be placed together. By staggering the stacks the row that needed access could slide right in between the other stacks. This made room for many more books in each section without sacrificing space. If they needed a book that was in the middle row the patrons had to ask the attendant to move the stacks as the way had to be clear of readers to move the stack. It was ingenious and the insurance company had pronounced it safe and effective. Bruce and Emmy were going to go far in their combined talents.

Finding all was well here Clark moved on. He avoided going to Sylvia's or Arabella's house because they were maniacs. The wedding plans were coming to a head and all stops had been pulled out. The wedding was next week and Andrew was chomping at the bit.

Twenty-Four

Same day

It was convenient that the ballroom at the Vermillion mansion could hold half the town because half the town had already accepted their invitation. Arabella and Sylvia had never been so busy or so excited. They had assumed that as they had both had just one boy each they would never get to plan a big beautiful wedding. Sylvia had been quite content to plan Clark and Thea's smaller wedding with Arabella's help because she was so glad that Clark had decided on one girl and was ready to settle down. She couldn't be more proud of her son and his family. Now Arabella was getting the same chance because Temple didn't care whether she had a big wedding or not and she and Andrew had given his mother and aunt carte blanche to make it fabulous. Arabella had political obligations as well as town and family to take into consideration and it was going to be a big bash. It was wonderful to have enough money to move heaven and earth to get the job done. Temple had been fitted and her attendants had been fitted and the gowns were straight out of a dream. Thea was her matron of honor of course and Emmy and Abby were bridesmaids along with four other of Temple's friends. Clark was best man and Bruce, Barry, Rance and three other colleagues of Andrew's were the ushers. The reception was planned down to the last olive and the flowers were going to keep the churches, nursing homes, and shut-ins happy for weeks after the wedding. The wedding cake was a masterpiece and big enough for the whole town to have a piece. The family had been avoiding Sylvia and Arabella like the plague and the women didn't have a care. They were organized and they knew it. Everything was ready and fabulous and they were content to go over everything one more time in case they had forgotten something.

Granger Sanderson and Frank Vermillion were happy to go about their business and let the women do the honors. They knew when the time came everything would be perfect. Their women were socialites after all and knew everyone and everybody. Granger had agreed to do the honors and officiate at the wedding as he had at Clark and Thea's; it had been memorable. Pastor Donahue would give a light sermon and the church was all prepared for the bride to walk down the flower-decked aisle. Patrick Phinney was to give the bride away as her surrogate father.

Across town the girls sat in the office of the beautifully refurbished library and talked about how beautiful the wedding was going to be. Andrew had eschewed a bachelor party, saying he didn't need to say goodbye to bachelorhood because he was going to be the happiest married man on the planet. Temple and the girls had agreed that showers and pre-wedding parties would be superfluous and were content to just look beautiful. Of course Arabella had already given each attendant a beautiful gift as a thank you for being part of the wedding and Temple and Thea were looking forward to being cousins and having their children be cousins. Emmy declared that she was feeling quite left out of the cousin department and Thea and Temple adopted her on the spot as their special cousin. Temple and Andrew would live in Temple's little house until theirs was finished being built. They were not in a hurry and Bruce's business was so busy he would need time. Temple and Andrew both agreed no one else could do their house but Emmy and Bruce and they would be glad to wait for them to find time. No two people could be happier and Temple was feeling the pinch. She was very superstitious and was totally ill at ease about being so happy. The killer and kidnapper were still out there and she was antsy that something would go wrong. Thea understood as she had been under the threat herself and they all tried to forget about unpleasant things and remained on the topic of the wedding and plans for Temple's house. She was throwing out ideas and Emmy was furiously taking notes. Emmy had to coax some pretty big changes in places because Temple was very conservative and not used to spending money hand over fist. She had about died when she learned that Andrew had lost three million dollars in ransom for her. He told her it was nothing but a drop in his fortune and she really quaked at being married to such a rich man. Thea and Emmy laughed and assured her she would never become spoiled and she felt better for having them as friends and said so. They both said they were the lucky ones to have her for a friend. It really was rare for more than two women to get along as well as the three of them did. Abby also fit real well into the scheme of things but couldn't be as carefree as they were because her schedule was so busy. Even though Olivia took up the slack with the children she still had her education and personal life to contend with. She was a busy lady. The girls smiled when they talked about the babies and Thea's household. They had all noticed when Perry and Olivia had come back to the patio at the barbeque how flushed and happy they had looked. They had been tending to the babies' nap time and apparently Perry must have finally got his courage up to address what everyone knew was a fact; that they were very attracted to each other. The girls were very happy for them and hoped they would be very happy together. They both deserved the best. Thea admitted to being selfish enough to want them to continue to live and work with her. She never thought of any of them as working for her. Her household ran like clockwork and yet nobody seemed to hurry or be locked into a strict regimen. Thea didn't want that to change but she loved her friends and wanted what was best for them as well. Her Uncle Perry was all that was left of her father's side except for a distant cousin and her son, and she loved Perry dearly. She loved Olivia too, even though she had known her just a short while, and the babies would be lost without her. Oh well, she wouldn't invite change until it happened.

Twenty-Five

Same day/the killer

    He had actually got an invite to the wedding. He had decided to stay around for a little bit to see what happened. His money was safe in a metal box and buried in his cellar. He still had plenty of time to go far, far away. He was really surprised to find out that Temple was alive and well. He must have been careless. He should have finished her when he had the chance, but she was so repulsive at the time. She was back to her beautiful self now but all he could remember was how she looked and smelled in that locked room. He was too fastidious for that type of thing. He had had to raise himself, no thanks to his drunk of a mother. Temple had reminded him of her, laying there in vomit and bodily fluids. He had seen his mother like that so often. Arty would clean her up until the next time. He didn't know how Arty could stand her, but he adored her even though she was a squalid drunk. Arty had come into their lives when he was twelve and he thought at first that it was going to be a good thing for him, but Arty didn't like kids and would like to have thrown him out onto the street, but his mother at least put her foot down on that. So he was lucky enough to stay and catch a beating if he so much as looked crossways at Arty or his mother. When he was eighteen he took off; best day of his life because he just happened to have skipped out with Arty's life savings. He still laughed when he thought about it. He wished he could have seen his face when he checked the old coffee can that he had buried in their back yard. He had watched Arty bury it one day and checked to see what it was. He kept it in mind and Arty kept adding to it. It was a tidy little sum by the time he left home. It bought him this house and paid for higher education that would make him a somebody someday. There was even some left over in the coffee can in the cellar. Then that bitch of a Carry had talked him into helping her break into the library to steal a fortune from the safe. He had gone to school with all of them and had met her again slumming in a bar and they had hit it off. She had been very accommodating and they hung out together when she wasn't with her ritzy friends. She didn't want him to meet them and after what happened in the library he was glad that he hadn't. He was smart, but she had misled him. She had said that there was a fortune just waiting to be picked. It wasn't until they were in the library office that she had told him she wanted to hold crummy manuscripts for ransom. He wanted fast cash and he told her so. He wanted Temple to notice him like he noticed her. Carry had laughed and said good luck with getting that expletive to notice the likes of him. She said she had been talking with Eric Scanlon a few times in Bar Harbor and he had bragged about Temple being the best he had ever had. Wait until she told that little tidbit. He had just seen red, grabbed the knife from the case, and she was dead before she hit the floor. He had almost decapitated her. Her mouth wouldn't diss anybody again. Eric was Temple's stepbrother for heaven's sake. He had thought fast and covered his tracks in a hurry. He was good at covering his tracks, he had had to do it all the time when he was a kid or he would have never survived. He had never seen so much blood; it just pumped right out of her in a gush. He was covered with it. He had grabbed a box of tissues from the desk and cleaned his shoes and glove. He even took the gloves off Carry to throw them off track. He then left by the same window that they came in by. It took him forever to clean his car and house after he got home. The clothes and shoes went into the landfill, never to be seen again. The look on that bitch's face was priceless when he slashed her. He didn't think that knife was so sharp. He would like to have kept it for himself. He liked nice things; he would get one of his own.

He saw her kissing that damned lawyer and the plan popped into his head fully formed. Kidnap her; ransom her. Sometimes it just worked better to act fast and he did. The note had been a stroke of genius; let them think he was ignorant and uneducated. He had scoured the town for a bolt hole if he ever needed one and now was the perfect time to use that old farmhouse. It had kind of backfired though because he had hit her too hard and she had messed herself and he didn't want her anymore. He wanted the money though and he got it. He laughed until the tears rolled down his cheeks. Boy, did he have the money. He would never be called a nobody again.

Twenty-Six

That same day

Andrew was in his office cleaning up details that would leave his agenda free for his honeymoon. He was the luckiest guy in the world and he knew it. He thanked God all the time for letting him get Temple back safe and sound. He was taking her to a secluded little island that his father had discovered years ago with Arabella and they had a small beach house there. It was paradise and he knew she would love it. He had pangs of fear every now and then that she wasn't safe. There was a man on duty twenty-four seven with her but she didn't know it. They were very discreet. He was taking no chances. She was in danger for some reason and his having money made her even a juicier target. She felt terrible about the ransom money but he would have given every penny he had to get her back safe. The kidnapper had underestimated the Vermillion fortune and might try again.

Clark had shared the information regarding Temple's stepbrothers with Andrew and Andrew had immediately hired Barry to put a man on watching them twenty-four seven as well. If they made a move toward Trafton, Andrew would know about it and take Temple away. He was practically living at Temple's house now; sleeping on the couch in her study. The little house was based loosely on Thea's original house in that it had a huge walk-in closet. Temple dressed simply but nicely and she was not a clothes horse. There was plenty of room for Andrew's extensive wardrobe of clothing. There was still a man on her house all the time so nobody could sneak up on them again. His bases were covered.

Barry was doing a tremendous job with his agency; keeping up with Clark's demands and now Andrew, and Frank was also thinking about hiring Barry's agency to replace his protective team. He had been impressed by the way they all worked together at the barbeque. Granger had already switched to them because they all knew his grandbabies and he didn't want them frightened.

Andrew looked at his watch and saw that it was time to pick up Temple, the best part of his day. He met up with Clark just as he was leaving and asked if there was any progress with the manhunt and Clark said not much. He waved to his cousin just as Clark answered his phone. Clark talked for a couple of minutes and Andrew knew something was drastically wrong so he waited for Clark to get off the phone.

"Go get Temple and don't let her out of your sight," he yelled as he jumped into his cruiser and tore off toward town with lights and siren blasting.

Andrew wasted no time with questions; he sped to the library in a red Porsche streak. He came to a screeching halt and met his watchman at the door. The watchman had been alerted by dispatch according to plan when anything popped up concerning the case. He quickly determined that Temple was fine and the girls were just leaving. Temple was setting the alarm and Emmy and Thea stopped to ask what was going on. Andrew couldn't tell them much of anything but they quickly used their phones to check on their loved ones as well. Thea knew that Clark would have called her if it concerned Rigby House or their entourage. Emmy called Bruce to check on him and he was about to leave his office as well. Thea quickly issued an invitation to all of them to come to Rigby House for one of Rene's famous meals. Tonight he was going to do just plain pot roast and what he couldn't do with pot roast wasn't worth mentioning. He always fed the entire compound and it was a great perk of the jobs. Rene was in his element cooking for a large crowd and yet having his own kitchen and answering to no one. He had complete authority over what was cooked and when. However, if someone needed a quick snack it was in front of them before they could blink. He cooked fabulous healthy meals—heavy on salads and fruit yet hearty for the men who needed to work hard at protecting his castle. "He rules with a heavy wooden spoon," Thea was known to say with a laugh.

The triplets were beginning to express their likes and dislikes to a certain extent and Olivia worked closely with Rene to keep them happy. Olivia, having raised multiples herself with her twins was a fountain of sage advice on how to turn them in another direction without causing a ruckus. She was a marvel.

Everyone accepted her invite and they traveled to Rigby in a convoy. Thea alerting Rene to the added company was grateful for his cheerful "good." Whenever Clark came in late or had to go out unexpectedly Rene was there with a hot meal for him when he came back. The whole compound ran on well-oiled wheels thanks to Perry and Olivia.

Twenty-Seven

Five o'clock Friday afternoon

Clark and his crew of fellow deputies pulled up to the Leighton Mansion gatehouse and the gate was wide open. A hysterical Hillary Leighton threw herself into Clark's arms and cried all over his uniform. She had blood on her shoes and legs and looked about ready to pass out. Clark handed her off to Betty Goodwin, one of his female deputies and walked in the open door of the mansion. Terry Wagner, one of Hillary's cronies, lay dead in the lush hallway. She too had died quickly with a slit throat and bled profusely. The butler sat on the bottom step of the elegant stairway and had been sick at his feet. His eyes were wet and he was in a bad way. The elderly butler was finding it hard to breathe and Clark quickly had the EMTs that had arrived on the scene tend to him. Terry Wagner was the friend that had seen Carry with a man in the black SUV. Like all of Hillary's friends she closely resembled Hillary. Her long blond hair was spread out in a fan where she had fallen.

Clark needed answers and Hillary had calmed down enough to hiccup her way through what she knew. Terry had seen a dark SUV that immediately jumped out to her as the one she had seen Carry in before she died. She had made the mistake of staring at the driver and he noticed her looking at him. She had quickly turned away and he thought it was Hillary. Carry had pointed Hillary out to him and told him who she was. He called Hillary and arranged to meet with her so they could figure out who had killed Carry. He simply identified himself as Carry's good friend and Hillary said to come over and she would leave the gate open. Terry arrived in the meantime and was telling Hillary about the SUV and what she had seen. Hillary said she knew all about it and he was coming over to talk with them about Carry's killer. She had told the butler to butt out and she would handle the door. She then went into the kitchen for snacks and told Terry to answer the door when Carry's friend rang the bell. She heard the bell and when she came into the hall a few minutes later, the door was wide open and Terry was lying in a bloody sprawl by the door. She screamed the house down and William had rushed in to be sick on the carpet. She called 911 and raced out of the house. She was afraid the killer was still in the house but saw the blood on the walk and realized he had left and she could be in danger. She was so glad to see Clark. He had gotten here so fast and she knew it was because he cared about her. Deputy Betty Goodwin rolled her eyes and continued to take notes.

Clark immediately issued an all points on any dark SUV seen in the area and the crime scene went to work on the hall and Terry's body was soon removed and her parents were notified by the sheriff. They were screaming about this being the second young woman killed viciously in Trafton and what was the sheriff going to do about it. The sheriff reckoned as there was a new lead and they would get to the bottom of this quickly. He left the parents of Terry Wagner and arrived back at the Leighton mansion in time for the body's removal. He was sick at heart and said so. William Peabody, the butler, had been given a sedative and was allowed to go to his room.

Clark told Hillary that she should also either leave to stay somewhere else for now or go to a farther point in the house and talk with her parents in Europe. He told her to use another exit and stay away from this hall for a few days. He told her to get someone to stay with her and she asked him if he couldn't do it.

"Hillary, listen to me," he said. "I am never going to care about you in that way, ever. Stop trying to convince yourself that it will be so. Even if I didn't love Thea with all my being, I would never love you. Just stop it Hillary and get over this mess you are in. You are in a great deal of trouble and the killer won't stop until he has gotten you or we catch him; now help us catch him if you can. What do you know that you haven't told us?"

Hillary shrank away from him at his harsh speaking and began to cry again. "I told you all I know except that Carry said he was an old friend that used to live here years ago and that he had always longed for Temple to pay attention to him; even back in high school he had loved her and followed her around like a lost puppy. I never could see the attraction but all the guys seemed to think she was adorable even back in grade school—even the high school guys followed her with their eyes. Carry said she had been in touch with Temple's stepbrothers and they had both bragged about having sex with her. Carry said when she was finished telling that around Temple wouldn't be so special. I told her I was afraid of the Scanlons and she better be careful; she just laughed. Do you think they did it, Clark?"

"Can you think of anyone else and anyone in particular that used to pine after Temple?" Clark asked.

"No, they all did, I tell you. We older girls used to watch her too, to see what she had that we didn't."

"Think hard and if you can come up with someone that moved away that cared about her, give me a call."

Clark then left to go home and get some rest and talk with Barry about it. He knew that Barry used to look after her like a big brother; maybe he would have some ideas.

He arrived at Rigby House to find quite a gathering in his kitchen and dining area and he was glad to see them. He sat wearily in a chair and told them all about Terry and Hillary. They were all shocked and they all tried to think of who it could be. Temple of course was oblivious because she had never noticed any undue attention. In her innocence she had always thought that the people just liked her—boys and girls.

Barry said that that was true, Temple hadn't a clue that she was special and had returned the boys flirting right back at them. It was part of her personality to be bouncy and flirty with everyone. She was just a people person and that was why she was so great at the library. The kids were drawn to her the same as the adults.

Temple cried out, "Do you mean I brought this on myself by flirting with this guy?"

"Of course not, Temple," Andrew said. "You can't change your personality just because some guy had delusions of grandeur. Look at how long I had to pine for you before you gave me the time of day. You are just you and everybody knows that. This guy is just a nutcase that thinks he can have you if he eliminates everyone else in the world."

"Am I really that callous of other people's feelings?" asked Temple.

Thea said, "Temple, you are not unfeeling of people, just the opposite. You love people and they know it. You bubble at them and they automatically respond to that—both sexes. Please don't ever change. There are so few of you in the world that it would be a pity for your personality to be affected by this episode. The only person in the town you have ever had words with is Andrew and we all knew it was because you thought he was special and you were fighting it. Just be Temple and we will all keep right on loving you."

Everyone else in the room agreed with Thea and surrounded her with their love. She gulped back tears and Andrew pulled her close.

Emmy suggested that they get the school yearbooks that were at the library for all the years that they were growing up and study them to see if anyone popped out at them.

"Good idea, Em," said Clark. "We will start on them tomorrow."

Barry said he would go see Patrick tomorrow and see if anyone stood out with him. He and Linda had kept an eye on Temple when she stayed with them and worked at the Gull. Maybe they might remember someone hanging around the restaurant. As Barry recalled most of the young boys who came in tripped over their own feet when they saw her anyway. Everyone laughed at that and Temple blushed.

With that they all agreed that tomorrow was going to come soon and they dispersed to go their various ways.

Barry told Andrew and Temple that their watchman had called that all was quiet at their house and they left knowing that they would be safe in their house. Thea offered rooms for them at Rigby House if they wanted to stay within the compound and they both said they didn't want to stop living their own lives. Andrew showed them the gun he had taken to carrying and he had shown Temple how to use the one she now kept at home as well. Barry gave Temple a little device that looked like a cell phone and showed Temple how to turn it on and use it. It was a stun gun and it might help her subdue anyone who got close enough to harm her.

Emmy and Bruce had gone earlier and that left just the folks that lived on the compound.

Clark had finished the delicious meal that had appeared magically before him when he sat down, and everyone went to bed.

Twenty-Eight

Eight o'clock the next morning/ the killer

He paced back and forth in a fury. He had to think. What if she had told anyone else about him? What was he going to do? "Don't panic!" he screamed at himself. He had taken care of it. It should be all right. He had to go get the paper; it would be in the paper. He went to his paper box and opened the paper. He tore through the paper and there was nothing there. "What the hell is going on?" There must be some way of finding out what was happening. He would go to his favorite diner; they always had the same old geezers gossiping. He rushed out of his house and headed for the little diner that all the good old boys frequented.

As usual Hap Sturgis was holding court at his table, and the killer sat at a nearby table after nodding at all the people in the place. They all knew him and he fit right in. He was a success story and they respected him.

Hap was talking about a murder that took place late yesterday afternoon. "Old man Leighton will probably tear right back from Europe," he said. "One thing after another since that girl was little. You'd think she would have learned something over the years. Probably have to have one of them forensic crews clean the place up. Pretty bloody I understand."

The killer left to go to the restroom. Hap's eyes followed him as he left the room, but he continued his story. "Don't know if the killer knew he had killed the wrong woman or not," he said. The killer came back into the room as the old timers got up and paid their bills. "Leave it to Hap to have the scoop," he thought. He ate his breakfast and left the diner a happy man.

He had cleaned his knife and put it with his money. He tossed the coverall that he had worn into the landfill and he was all clear on that. He had purchased his new knife in Portland and it was just as sharp as the one at the library. He really liked the way it felt. He really liked the way it felt to slash a pretty girl's throat; it turned him on just thinking about it. He might have to kill again.

Twenty-Nine

Nine o'clock the same morning

Temple opened up the library and Andrew had her bodyguard stay right in the library today. The guard sat right behind the reception desk and pretended to work on some papers. Andrew went on his way with a few words of caution and love. Thea and Emmy arrived at the same time and the girls took down the yearbooks and began to peruse them for any guys that jumped out as weird. It would take a while as they were all weird according to Emmy. They laughed at the hairstyles on the girls and guys and gossiped about various people that had gotten married over the years and to whom.

After several hours of looking the girls had not found anyone that jumped out at them. The whole town was there in one way or another—teachers, cousins and friends. Several had gone away for a while and then come back. That seemed to be the trend for Trafton; everyone wanted to leave but wasted no time in coming back to raise a family with a hometown girl.

Webster came to work in the afternoon and they asked him if he could think of anyone that they hadn't and he said he would have to think on it; he would ask Mr. Severied, too. Webster was dating a local girl and he knew everybody.

Clark came by to see if they had made any progress with some suspects and they had to tell him that nobody fit the description of a killer to them. He thanked them and left.

Thea and Emmy left shortly after and it was quiet in the library for a while.

Emmy stopped in at the supermarket to do the week's shopping. There wasn't a bean in her house. She met a number of people that she knew and pondered on how odd it was to know all these people well. She would swear that they were all kind, nice people. She had known most of the people in town her whole life.

How could you pick a killer out of them when they were all friends and acquaintances?

At the check-out counter she talked with Penny Randolph. Penny was one of the guys who had left town and returned to be successful. He owned the little market and was one of the happiest people Emmy knew. Pennington Randolph had grown up poor as a church mouse and had struggled his whole life. His family had moved away and he was gone for a few years. He had come into some money and used it wisely. He was educated and happy. Everyone knew and liked Penny and Penny's Market seemed to be thriving. There were all kinds of stories just like his. Emmy recalled that Penny had been secretly in love with Temple just like Ralph Myers in the next aisle. Ralph nodded to Emmy and asked her how she was doing. She chatted with him about nothing important while she wondered if Ralph could be the one. He had come back to Trafton just a year ago and was living by himself. He had opened a small insurance office and reportedly was successful too. Archie Collins came up behind Emmy and asked how Bruce was doing. Archie was the town's biggest flirt and he too had just come back to town a few years ago and he had been in love with Temple. As far as Emmy knew Temple had tolerated Archie's passes with little attention and he knew she would break his arm if he followed through on his suggestions. He commented to Ralph and Penny that Bruce was a lucky son of a gun to have captured Emmy and she gathered her cart and left to load her groceries in her car. Ralph walked out with her and asked her if she needed any help and she said she was fine.

"How is Temple doing? I heard she was kidnapped and treated badly," he said. "She is a proud woman. It must have been hard for her."

"Ralph, it would have been hard on any woman, proud or otherwise. She is doing fine, thank you for asking. Her wedding is in a few days and she is very busy of course."

Emmy watched Ralph in her rear view mirror as she drove away. Odd that he should comment on Temple's ordeal. As far as she knew the details had been kept very quiet; even she didn't know the whole story. She would have to ask Temple about Ralph.

Thirty

Later that same day

Barry stopped at the Gull for lunch and talked with Patrick and Linda Phinney about the guys that used to hang out there when Temple worked for them. Linda said, "There was a whole table of them. They would stay for hours just sipping on one coke just so they could watch Temple. She was oblivious to them. She treated them all just like they were her good friends and nothing more. Do you remember who they were, Patty?"

"Well, let me see, it all runs together after a while. I remember that Penny Randolph had it bad and so did Mr. Wonderful, Archie Collins," Patrick said.

"Oh, and don't forget Ralph Meyers and Owen Pratt and several others," Linda said. "They all vied for her attention."

"Thanks for your suggestions. I remember now how they would clown to make her laugh," Barry said. "We'll check out everybody."

Barry's next stop was the library and he asked Temple about the guys at the table and she laughed at the memory of some of their antics. Webster said not to forget Harlan Madden; he was the funniest of them all. They talked some more but couldn't come up with anyone else and Barry said he would see them at the wedding. That was two days away.

Barry ran into Clark at the sheriff's department and gave him some names. Clark said Emmy had given him most of the same names a few minutes ago. He said she had run into some of them at Penny's Market and the more she thought about it the more she felt she should call him. He would check them out for scuba experience.

Just as they were leaving, Thea pulled up in her armored SUV and she had all three little lords in the rear with Mrs. McMillian and Perry. Thea's vehicle was followed as always by a black SUV with two security personnel in full protection mode. She said they were on their way to the Gull for lunch and would like their daddy to join them. Clark laughed and said he thought that could be arranged and he and Barry joined the convoy to the Gull where they were greeted by Linda and Patrick with big smiles and the promise of a great dessert if they were good boys and ate all of their lunch.

Thea had phoned ahead for a table and three orders of baby burgers and baby fries. She only allowed them these treats on special occasions and Rene frowned his disapproval when the boys shrieked about it. He was right in guessing that she would allow them to share a whoopie pie as well.

The adults all ordered the same in a larger portion and a good time was had by all. Perry and Mrs. McMillian sat to the side and enjoyed their family having so much fun. Barry had to leave first and he instructed his very stuffed security crew to be on the watch and went back to Rigby House. The family outing was soon breaking up as three little boys were very sleepy after their whoopie pie dessert.

Clark kissed his family good-bye and they all left for home. He thanked God for his wonderful luck and family. He wondered if Thea had told anyone yet that the boys would have a brother or sister in a few months. Of course Abby already knew as she had told them long before they knew for sure. "That woman is a marvel," he thought.

Thea had in fact told Emmy, but she didn't want to steal Temple's thunder by announcing it before Temple's wedding and she had told nobody else, especially Sylvia. They would find out all in good time.

Thea had stopped at Sylvia's on the way to the outing and they had had a good visit and Sylvia said everything was all set for the wedding. The triplets loved to visit with Granger and Sylvia and they spoiled them rotten. The boys always ran to their playroom to see what their grandparents had bought for them. Sylvia would be happy to hear she was having another grandchild.

Thirty-One

Later that evening

Emmy had prepared a special supper for Bruce. Her larder was full and she had a lot of items to choose from. He arrived on time and had brought some champagne. They laughed at their good fortune to have their business thriving. They dined well and finished with a nice bread pudding. They did the dishes together and when they were finished Bruce took Emmy's hand and led her out on the front porch. There was a huge package sitting there with a red bow on it. Emmy was surprised and asked him what it was.

"Open it and see," he said.

Emmy tore the wrappings off the box and found another box inside that one. She did the same thing for a total of ten boxes. In the last box was a little velvet jewelry box and inside that box was a huge diamond ring. She turned around to look at Bruce and he was on his knees behind her. "Will you marry me Emmy, please?"

Emmy sank to her knees in front of him with stars in her eyes. "Yes, yes, yes," she cried and flung her arms around his neck.

"I wanted to wait until the business was well off the ground and I could afford to treat you right," he said. "I hope you hadn't given up on me as husband material."

"No, my darling, I had faith that you would ask in your own good time. I wish I could call everyone right now and tell them; you know that I can't for three whole days, don't you?" she asked.

"Yes, I am sorry Em, I just didn't think about it at the time. It will be our secret if you like," he said.

"No, I simply have to call Thea. We already share one secret until after the wedding anyway," she said. "Thea and Clark are going to have another baby."

"Wow, that is good news! Just don't get me married off until I get used to being engaged, okay love? This crowd tends to get married quickly."

"Don't worry my sweet; I intend to have everything just right when we tie the knot. I love you so much, Mr. Garrett," Emmy said.

"I love you too, Ms. Harrison," Bruce said.

Emmy got on the phone to Thea.

"Thea I know everyone thought Bruce and I were engaged before, but we weren't officially, now we are! He just asked me and gave me a huge diamond. It will have to be our secret until after the wedding though."

"Of course, Em! I am so happy for you! You will have to tell me all about it tomorrow when we have our Friday lunch. Now we have two secrets my friend," said Thea.

"Hey, Thea, speaking of secrets, how did Ralph Meyers know that Temple had been through an ordeal with her kidnapping?" Emmy asked.

"I am afraid I might have mentioned how frightened she was when I spoke to him the next day. I was talking about insurance and real estate with him and he mentioned he had heard about Temple and I said yes it was an awful ordeal for her. Is he telling it around, Em?"

"No, he just mentioned it in passing at the market and I wondered. Did you get the insurance for the library all settled?" Em asked.

"Yes, but he is branching out into real estate and I am looking for some property on the water, preferably a large peninsula like mine. I am interested in that huge stretch of ocean front that is the next cove over from us at Rigby House. I think there might be a need for some new housing in the near future. I know that Andrew just bought the entire cove and land to our right and I am looking to buy to the left of us. It would tie up that whole stretch of water for our families. Wouldn't that be wonderful?"

"Yes, I knew about Andrew's property. Bruce and I have been scouting for the best location on the site for their house. It is going to be magnificent, Thea," Emmy said.

"I can't wait for the wedding on Saturday. It is going to be the biggest bash of the year here in Trafton. Isabella and Sylvia have outdone themselves," Thea said.

Thirty-Two

Friday morning, Rigby House

Abby walked into the kitchen just as Barry was getting up to leave. He promptly sat back down. He had been hanging around for the last hour waiting for her to come down. She had helped Olivia get the babies fed and bathed for the morning and now she was on her way to school. She would be so glad to graduate in two weeks. She hoped everyone would attend her graduation. She had worked very hard to keep her grades up and was glad it would be over and she could get on with her life. She said as much to Barry and Rene and they grunted non-committally. They had all been sworn to secrecy by Thea and it was hard to keep a straight face in front of Abby. Thea had a party planned that would knock Abby's socks off and she wanted it to be a surprise. It was easy to get organized because Abby was away so much. They had to be careful what they said in front of the babies because they were at an age where they told everything they knew with pleasure. They were all pretty sure that Abby didn't have an inkling to what they were doing. Barry walked her out to her car and asked her shyly if he could take her to dinner in Portland that evening.

"Why, Barry," she mocked in a Temple fashion. "I didn't know you cared."

Barry looked her in the eye and, disregarding her flippancy, said, "I care Abby, I care."

Abby was visibly shaken as she got in her car.

"Yes or no?" Barry said.

Abby looked at him and said, "Yes."

Abby drove off in a daze and Barry went about his business about ten feet off the ground. He had been so nervous to tell her that he cared about her and he hoped he hadn't blown it. She seemed to take it in her stride, but with Abby it was hard to tell.

Abby in the meantime arrived in Portland with no idea of how she had gotten there. She had been on auto pilot thinking about what Barry had said to her. "Was he serious? Did he want to make their friendship more personal?" She had been attracted to him from the start but had kept it very low key and flirty. She had hoped when Rance had started to show a little interest that he would step up to the plate, but he had seemed perfectly content to share her attention with Rance and the others. Barry was so deep that it was hard to know what he was thinking. She just knew she couldn't wait for tonight to come.

She went into class and didn't hear a word her professor said. She tuned in after a while and had to scramble to catch up with the others. She needed to forget Barry and pay attention or she wouldn't be graduating. She had crammed so many classes into the two years of attending that her head was spinning but it was worth it. Her education was giving her loads of confidence and she was so glad Thea had come drooping into her rest area on that fateful day.

Thea was pregnant again and they were delighted. They had asked her not to mention it until after the wedding and she wouldn't but she was so glad for them. They were the best parents in the world. In spite of their busy days they managed to give the little boys quality attention and love. It would be easy to palm them off on the nanny, but they did their share of cleaning up and feeding as well as getting soaked in the bath. The boys were darling because of the love they received from everyone. She noticed that Barry seemed to care an awful lot for the little tykes and she hoped that... "Stop that," she thought. "Don't even go there."

With a huge effort she pulled herself together and thought about her class work—almost.

Thirty-Three

Friday morning at the library

Temple and her entourage of bodyguards arrived promptly at eight o'clock. Andrew had upped the protection until he could get her out of the country after the wedding. He wasn't taking any chances. They would have guards fly with them to their destination and hang in the background for their honeymoon; it was unfortunate but necessary.

Temple was so excited that she just sat and stared into space. Everyone laughed when they had to ask her something twice. They could understand her distraction. She was getting married at four o'clock tomorrow and to the man she had loved at a distance for years. She kept pinching herself; she would be a mass of black and blues if she didn't stop.

Emmy stopped by to offer her moral support and Thea was close behind. Barry came in as they were chatting about the rehearsal dinner that night and he swallowed hard and left quickly.

"What was that all about?" Emmy asked.

"I think he forgot about the dinner," Thea said "He needs to change some plans I guess. I saw him talking to Abby this morning out in the drive and they both looked shaken. Keep your fingers crossed, ladies," she grinned.

Wow, they had both forgotten about the rehearsal dinner! What could he do now? He would have to wait for her to come home to find out what to do. Barry drove slowly back to Rigby House completely forgetting what he had come to ask Temple about. He had wanted some advice about how to approach Abby for a more serious relationship. Come to think of it she was probably not the person to ask about expediting a relationship; it had taken her and Andrew years to get to the talking stage.

Barry had almost reached Rigby House compound when his cell phone rang. It was Victor Leighton and he wanted complete protection for his house and daughter around the clock starting right now. He said he had heard that Barry's security firm was one of the best in New England and money was no object. He told Barry he was in Europe for an extended stay and couldn't get away to come home right now and his daughter had filled him in on all that was happening at home; if the police couldn't do their job then he wanted her to be protected.

Barry had pulled over to the side of the road and told Victor Leighton the terms of his contract. One of the important items that he stressed to Leighton was that his men would take no lip from Hillary and if she insisted on doing it they would be instructed to walk off the job. Leighton said he would call her right now and tell her that she was to keep her mouth shut to the security team and let them do their job.

Barry made arrangements for a man to go there immediately and start the process of setting up a twenty-four seven watch. It was a good thing he had hired ten new men this month and their training was complete. All of his personnel needed police training plus Barry's own special brand of security training. He was the best and he knew it.

He paced the floor in the security complex until he saw Abby pull into the gate and he went out to intercept her. She saw his concerned look and thought, "I knew it, he is going to cancel!"

Barry opened her passenger door and folded his large body into the seat.

"We need to talk, Abby," he said.

"No problem, Barry. If you want to cancel dinner, I understand," Abby said.

"Abby, I want to go to dinner with you in the worst way, but we both forgot that the rehearsal dinner is tonight and we both need to attend," Barry said.

Abby let out a huge sigh. "Oh gosh, Barry, I totally forgot. We can go some other time, okay?"

"Let's make it a date for Sunday night right now. I don't want Rance to beat me to it tomorrow at the wedding. Will you partner with me tomorrow, Abby?" Barry asked.

She pulled her little SUV up the drive to the door and Barry got out and she continued on to the garage complex. She was totally on cloud nine, but how could she have forgotten the rehearsal dinner. She really was rattled. She rushed into the house and up to her suite; she intended to knock Mr. Applegate's socks off tonight.

Thirty-Four

The rehearsal dinner Friday evening.

Patrick Phinney had closed his restaurant for the dinner and arranged one enormous table to accommodate the wedding party. Arabella had paid him well and he and Linda were doing their best to make it a success. He was in the wedding after all as "father" of the bride and they had pulled out all stops. The food was wonderful and his staff would serve it with aplomb.

The parking lot began to fill up as the wedding party arrived one after the other. It was a large group of people that gathered in the restaurant to be seated. The others watched with interest as Abby and Barry came in together and rearranged the seating to accommodate them sitting together. Though Abby blushed at the amused looks of the others she couldn't help but glow at the attention from Barry. The noise level in the restaurant was rising steadily and Arabella asked everyone to please be sure to go right to the rehearsal as soon as they were finished. Everyone thoroughly enjoyed their meal and the cars all left together to go to the church for the final rehearsal.

Clark and Rance had arranged for some reserve officers to fill in for them so they could attend the dinner and rehearsal. They all hoped they could get through the wedding without any serious calls taking them away.

The rehearsal went off with only minor glitches and everybody agreed it was going to go well tomorrow afternoon for the wedding.

They were all standing on the church steps chatting when Clark had to answer his cell phone. He had just turned it back on and it was dispatch.

One of the reserve officers had responded to a call for help at the marina where Hap Sturgis had his little business. When the officer arrived he found a badly hurt Hap lying on the deck of a nearby boat.

Hap was unconscious and had lost a lot of blood from a head wound. They had rushed him to the emergency room and the EMTs said he had come around long enough to ask for Clark right away.

Clark put on the siren and lights and wasted no time in going to the hospital. Sylvia and Granger were close behind as Hap was Sylvia's cousin.

Hap was in surgery to relieve pressure on his brain and they waited anxiously in the waiting area for him to get out of surgery. Clark couldn't imagine who would hurt Hap. He was a fixture around Trafton that everybody loved. He knew everyone and everything. Clark was sorry he had asked Hap to keep his eyes peeled; he could just see him getting into trouble trying to find out who had kidnapped Temple. It was going to be a long night.

When the doctor came to the waiting room he said Hap was holding his own but it would be a few days before they would know if he was going to make it.

"He is strong and healthy as a horse, but he took an awful blow to the head," the doctor said.

Clark had Rance and his best men at the scene trying to piece together what had happened and to preserve any evidence they could find. He didn't hold out much hope. He wished he could be there but he didn't want to leave in case Hap regained consciousness.

Thea arrived with a care package from Rene and they all relished the good sandwiches and hot coffee that Rene had prepared especially for them.

At about one o'clock a.m. Sylvia, Granger and Thea left with a promise to return later in the day before the wedding. Clark sat in a chair in Hap's room and listened to the beep of the monitors and thought about how much he loved the old man that had taught him how to sail and handle any kind of boat in the marina when he could hardly walk. He loved hanging out with Hap. It was exciting to hear his stories, and as a kid he played pirate with Hap. Clark dozed in the chair but was alert for any movement from the bed. A guard was posted at the door and would be there until Clark knew what was going on.

Rance had called earlier to tell Clark that they couldn't see much in the dark even with the crime scene lights so they were going to secure the scene and then be there again at first light.

Hap did some stirring around and mumbling during the night but he didn't regain full consciousness. Clark knew he wanted to tell him something and he didn't want to leave his side, but he would have to leave around three to get ready for the wedding. He didn't want this incident to ruin Andrew's wedding. Thea arrived back at the hospital around eight o'clock with some fresh clothes for Clark and a hearty breakfast from Rene. She told him she would bring his tux and wedding apparel if Hap hadn't recovered consciousness by the time he had to leave and that would save a little time.

Clark's men at the scene had found nothing to indicate that Hap had been attacked on the boat or the pier other than the puddle of blood that he had been lying in. His friend Willie Leach had found him and then Willie had disappeared after calling the ambulance for Hap. Hard telling what Willie was up to.

The morning wore on and Hap continued to mumble Clark's name. It was frustrating for Clark but the doctor didn't want Hap to be rushed to consciousness—he wanted him to arrive there on his own right now. He said if he didn't come around in a day or two they could then try some stimulant to try and wake him. The swelling had gone down quite a bit and the x-rays looked good according to the doctor.

Sylvia came in to see if there was any improvement and left after a short while; they had so much to do. The women were all at the hairdressers' and Isabella had enlisted two salons to work on the wedding party. Everything was all ready except for Hap, he had wanted to see Temple get married to Andrew and now he would miss it. He would have to settle for the supreme video that Arabella was having done of the wedding along with the professional photographer's pictures.

At one o'clock Hap opened his eyes and looked at Clark. "I knew you would come, Clark. I thought I could help you out a little but he snuck up on me. Should have told you what I was doing."

"Hap, don't tire yourself, take your time but I really need to know who did this to you?"

"Just give me a minute to get my thoughts straight, son," Hap said.

Clark rang for the nurse and the doctor came in to check him out. He looked in Hap's eyes and pronounced him as hard headed as ever. "Don't tire him too much, Clark, but I know you need to talk to him," the doctor said.

Hap was fidgeting and wanting to get down to business. He told Clark what had happened and Clark jumped up ready to go and arrest the killer.

Thirty-Five

Ten o'clock Saturday morning/ the killer

What happened? How did he get here; where ever here was. His head hurt like white blazes and he was in a pool of filthy stinking water. He needed to go to the bathroom and his hands and feet were tied. His hands were behind him so he couldn't see what was binding him but he knew it was tight. It was almost totally dark and he could see that he was in the bilge of a boat, probably a lobster boat. He couldn't hear anything so he knew he was not at the dock. The last thing he remembered was getting out of his car at his house after he had killed that old bastard Hap Sturgis. Hap had brought it on himself.

"Hell, I actually liked the old bastard; everybody did, but it was him or me."

He had met me after work and asked me if he could borrow my scuba gear; his leer told me he knew all about me. I tried to bluff it out and told him I didn't know how to scuba dive and he was mistaken, but he just smiled and said okay and left. I knew he was on to me and I knew he had to go. I crept up behind him in the dark on the pier and used my tire iron to finish him off. He dropped into the oily water between the boats like a rock. I heard him splash when he hit the water and then I got the hell out of there. Then I tore home in a hurry to establish an alibi with my neighbor. That's when the lights went out. He wondered who had hit him and why.

A ruckus on deck alerted him to the fact that someone had come on board. Two men came slowly down the ladder in the corner and they were carrying a pail. They both had scarves around their faces and were dressed like fishermen. They had to crouch when they came over to him and one said, "Well, looky there, I think the snake is awake."

The other one said, "Yeah, let's give him something to eat."

They then dumped the contents of the pail down the front of his shirt. It smelled like a combination of chum and the head's contents.

He gagged and tried to scream for help, but his throat was so dry all that came out was a squeak.

The men laughed and went back up the ladder taking the pail with them.

"Don't worry we'll bring you some more supper later," one laughed.

What was he going to do? He couldn't bear to sit in this filth, he would rather be dead. He cried and screamed in his head but it didn't bring him any relief and the ultimate humiliation was when he added his own body waste to the water. His hysterical reaction almost brought him the blessed relief he sought, but he only fainted and slumped against the side of the boat.

Thirty-Six

Hap's story

'When you told me about poor little Temple and asked me to keep my eyes open, I decided to do just that. I went over to that old farmhouse on Lois Lane and checked it out. I found the filthy bed and knew that that skunk had made that beautiful little girl sit in that mess. I determined to find him no matter what as a favor to Sherri. Before I could do much sleuthing there was another killing at the Leighton house. I figgered it was the same guy doing all of these dreadful things.

"I was sitting at Rafe's Café talking with the boys over breakfast and everybody in the place thought I had the inside scoop because of you, so I began telling them what I knew; I didn't tell them you never tell me anything juicy. I talked about old man Leighton having to hire a forensic crew to clean up all that blood and gore and darned if the young fella at the next table didn't git up and go to the head. Now I wondered what kind of a fella would git up and leave when I was telling such a gory tale. I hadn't got to the part where he killed the wrong girl and it's a good thing because he probably would have rushed right over to finish Hillary off. Anyhow, I figgered he didn't need to hear my story because he already knew what had happened. Right then and there I was pretty sure I had my man. I talked with a few friends about it and they figgered I was on the right track, so I decided to go see him and ask him if I could borry his scuba equipment. He jumped like a scalded cat and denied having any and didn't know what I was talking about. I said 'ayup' and left. I planned on telling you all this but you was at that supper and I thought I'd wait until the wedding and tell you there and you could arrest him right after. I never made it. I was walking down the pier checking the boats that had come in, and I had tied up *The Mary Lucinda* earlier and wanted to check her fender. I heard the step behind me a second too late and 'crack' the roof fell in. I wasn't quite out and I caught the bow line on

Mary as I went by and moved hand over fist to the bow of the boat and 'walked' up the side and hoisted over the rail. I had made a hell of a splash with my feet as I hit the water and he thought I had gone under. But I had used up all my strength and I passed out right there on the deck. My pals had heard me cry out and came to see what was wrong. I came to long enough to tell them to call you and tell who it was that had done it. I guess after the boys called you folks they disappeared. They aren't too fond of the law in a lot of ways. I'm sorry, Clark, I won't tell you who they were. But I can tell you who hit me and who I am pretty sure is the killer," and he did.

Thirty-Seven

Two O'clock Saturday

Clark took his team to the house of the man that Hap had said was the killer and nobody answered the door. He asked the neighbors if they had seen him and they said that he had come home around eight and then another vehicle took off right about that time. They hadn't bothered to look so they couldn't help him there.

Based on what Hap had said, Clark asked Granger for an emergency search warrant and the judge obliged. They searched the house and found fresh turned earth in the cellar. They dug up the ransom money, a knife and a can with some money in it. Clark immediately put out an all points on the killer and they got the knife to forensics.

Rance had verified that Carry had been talking to the Scanlons on the land line at her father's house and Clark thanked him for the update. It was a moot fact at this point, but they would get back to the Scanlon boys at another time. Right now they had to find out where the killer was.

Thirty-Eight

The wedding

Clark and Rance raced to their houses and got dressed for the wedding and made it with time to spare. By tacit agreement they weren't going to tell Temple who the killer was, but Thea said she should know to be on the lookout for him. Clark told her to tell Temple when she went to the dressing room of the bride and he would tell Andrew.

Temple was shocked to hear who had kidnapped her and killed Terry and Carry, but she wasn't going to let him spoil her wedding. Thea told her he was still on the loose and she said they would watch for him. A guard was watching their plane right now and they were going straight there after the reception.

The wedding was sensational and the whole town was pleased—well, most of the town anyway.

When the wedding march started and Temple walked down the aisle to take Andrew's hand, with her entourage following, there wasn't a dry eye in the church. They exchanged vows that they had written themselves and Granger and Pastor Donahue actually shared the wedding ceremony in a way that was so beautiful and touching it would be remembered for a long time.

The reception was lavish and the honeymooning Mr. and Mrs. Andrew Vermillion left in a cloud of bird seed for the airport with no interruptions from the killer. Frank's private jet took the blissfully happy couple to their island getaway and four happy guards had an unexpected vacation on a remote island hideaway.

The guards were housed with the couple that kept the house ready for the family at all times. There were plenty of rooms in the carriage house for them and Andrew carried his bride across the threshold and kicked the door shut behind him. He had left orders that a meal should be prepared and that no one was to disturb them until asked.

They took their picnic meal out onto the lanai and just looked at each other. Temple was shy but Andrew didn't rush her in any way. She went into the bathroom off their bedroom and bathed in a luxurious bubble bath. She came out with her long black curly hair down her back and wearing a beautiful white peignoir set that made Andrew glad he had showered in another bathroom. He met her halfway and kissed her gently. He set off a conflagration that took them both by surprise and they made it to the king size bed and dropped down. Andrew kissed her and slowly removed her negligee; he was already naked, having worn nothing but a towel from the other bath. Temple's shyness soon vanished under Andrew's soft touch. When Andrew called out her name in a paroxysm of joy, Temple was thinking she was rather sorry she had waited so long and Andrew was thinking, "Boy, was that worth the wait!"

They had two weeks to enjoy the fabulous and exciting exploration of each other's bodies and they wasted no time in doing so.

The guards were going to have a boring time in paradise.

Thirty-Nine

Back at Rigby House Saturday evening

Barry thought he had never seen such a beautiful sight as Abby walking down the aisle next to him at the church. All of the attendant women had their hair up in elaborate old fashion and they were all beautiful but, as far as Barry was concerned, nobody could touch Abby.

Clark was having the same thoughts about Thea, and Bruce touched Emmy's hand to let her know he was thinking of their own wedding.

They were all back at Rigby House trying to map out a reason for the killer to do what he did, but could find no rational explanation. They also wondered where he was.

Barry was holding Abby's hand in what was, for him, a bold display of affection. More than one smile was concealed in the room. As usual they were in Rene's huge kitchen and being fed with a scrumptious meal.

Perry had shyly kissed Olivia on the cheek when they came home. She had elected to stay with the boys as she hadn't known Temple that long and Perry had reluctantly gone without her; now they were staying close to each other.

"What a house of love," thought Thea. "I hope it always stays this way." She reached out and took her own husband's hand and he put it on her stomach and smiled.

Clark cleared his throat and said, "We have an announcement to make, loved ones. Thea and I are going to be adding a brother or sister to the ménage in the fall and we hope you are all as thrilled as we are as it will mean more work for you all. We hope we can make a smooth transition with the new baby and everyone will continue with us."

There were assents all around and Clark and Thea thanked each and every one for their service and devotion to the boys.

Forty

In The Bilge/The Killer

How can I stand this? Will those bastards kill me? I wish they would. I have never suffered like this even when Arty McMillian left his wife and kids and moved in with my mother. His kids were the lucky ones—they had a decent mother.

They had come back three times and each time they had dumped more stinking waste on him. He had been here three days and all they had given him was a couple of small drinks of stagnant water and a couple of bites of moldy bread. He had asked them why they were doing this and they just said, "What goes around comes around, fella. We want you to get what's coming to you before you get molly-coddled in prison. You ought to survive a few more days of our hospitality. What's the matter, snake? You don't like living like this?"

He heard them come on deck and he shuddered; more filth to be dumped on him. His hands and feet were numb and he wanted to die. When they came crouching over to him this time they didn't have a pail. They hunkered down and looked at him. He said, "If you let me go I will give you each a million dollars in cash."

The two men threw back their heads and laughed, "Well now son, you don't have that money anymore. You see Hap told them who you were and they went to your house and found it along with the murder weapon you used on poor Terry, so you are as poor as a church mouse, chummy. All they have to do is come and collect you now. We are tired of babysitting your ugly smelly face."

"You're lying," he screamed. "I killed Hap, I heard him hit the water after I bashed him with my tire iron. I have the money I got for kidnapping Temple and you can have all of it, just let me go." He sobbed that he had been seeing Carry and Terry and they came and sat with him and asked him why he had killed them. "Please, let me go," he sobbed.

"Well, what do you think?" said one of the men. "Should we let him go?"

"Yup," said the other as he clicked something in his pocket. "I guess it's time."

They had on long rubber fishing gloves and they dragged him to the ladder and dragged him up to the deck of the boat. He still couldn't see their faces as they still were covered by scarves. One of them started the boat and the other made a call on his cell phone.

"Tell Lieutenant Clark Sanderson that Webster Adams is on Hap Sturgis's dock. He'd better get there right away. There's a tape recording in Hap's shack that might interest him, too."

About the Author

Delia Drake is a Maine author who enjoys telling Maine stories. This is her second book in the cousin series and she hopes you all enjoy her humble efforts. She is assisted in her ramblings by her fur babies; Rachel Rose Brann, a big black cat; and Paisley Honeybee Brann, a beautiful Pomeranian.

www.ingramcontent.com/pod-product-compliance
Lightning Source LLC
Chambersburg PA
CBHW052205170626
46812CB00004B/1663